THE IMMORTAL BARTFUSS

THE
IMMORTAL
BARTFUSS

Aharon Appelfeld

 TRANSLATED FROM THE HEBREW
BY JEFFREY M. GREEN

Weidenfeld & Nicolson
LONDON

First published in Great Britain in 1988 by
George Weidenfeld & Nicolson Limited
91 Clapham High Street, London SW4 7TA

ISBN 0 297 79272 5

Printed in Great Britain by
Redwood Burn Limited, Trowbridge, Wiltshire

THE IMMORTAL BARTFUSS

1

Bartfuss is immortal. In the Second World War he was in one of the smaller of those notorious camps. Now he's fifty, married to a woman he used to call Rosa, with two daughters, one married. He has a ground-floor apartment, not very large, with two trees growing at the entrance.

Every day he rises at the same time, a quarter to five. At that hour he still manages to take in the half-light of the morning, the fog, and the quiet before everyone gets up. In the other room, separated by a long corridor, his wife and younger daughter sleep together in the double bed. They get up late, and at this hour they are plunged deep in slumber. So he closes the door between them to muffle the noise a little.

He drinks a cup of coffee and lights a cigarette right away. The first cigarette makes him feel very good. For a long while he sits next to the window and absorbs the little tremors of the morning: an old man walks to synagogue, a truck unloads a crate of milk. These little sights charm his eyes.

At six he rises, gets to his feet, lights a second cigarette, and, to his surprise, discovers some unpleasant scraps of food in the sink. The old fury rises in him immediately. But he doesn't let the fury take control of him. The muscles tense sharply, in his neck for some reason, and he nips his anger in the bud. He goes straight to his room.

His room is practically bare: just a bed, a chair, and a cupboard. When he does his accounts he sits on the bed and uses the chair as a desk. Once Rosa tried to dress up the walls a little. She even brought in a table and chairs. That was years ago, when they still talked. Bartfuss cleared them right out, with his own hands.

Since then the room has stood bereft of any garment. If not for the few shadows that creep in through the shutters, white glare would cover everything. In contrast, Rosa's room is crammed full of colored pictures and vases. The pictures spread over the entire wall with their colors: golden girls swimming in greenery.

"What do you have against them?" she asked years ago, when she was still young and the girls were only children.

"I don't know."

"Isn't the greenery pleasing? The girls are nature girls."

Even then he didn't like discussions. But the expression "nature girls" revolted him. He didn't know what to say, just: "I don't know." His reactions, though they were few, always provoked Rosa's tongue. She seemed to await them. She always rushed in to explain, to dispel, to pile words upon words. She loved the pictures and she passed that love on to her daughters. Since then, years have passed and his words have grown fewer. Now he hardly talks, nor does he get angry. It's been years since he got angry. Recently he's learned to ignore, at least to pretend. Now there is a tacit competition between them: who will ignore most.

At seven he locks his room and goes out into the corridor. At that hour Rosa wakes up too. She lies in bed and eavesdrops on him with her eyes closed. That eavesdropping, which he senses, hastens his movements. He hurries out.

At seven the street is empty. The sea and the morning lights dissipate the last remains of his staleness. He halts and imagines the way Rosa gets up, the words she spouts into space. Then he stops doing that. He stands near the sea and no absent vision distracts him. The sea bathes him in cool breezes.

At eight he is already sitting in the café. At that hour the proprietor isn't particularly accommodating, but Bartfuss feels at ease because he's a regular customer. The second cup of coffee, the eight o'clock coffee, arouses his senses, and his sight gets sharper. For a long time he sits without uttering a syllable. The sight isn't especially breathtaking—the sink is full of dishes, yesterday's cups are on the counter—but the transistor radio isn't roaring. He invested substantial effort into silencing that frightful music. At last they'd agreed not to play music in the morning.

He sits by himself. For about two hours he is by himself. During that time he has thoughts. It would be better without those thoughts, but you can't repress them completely. Unavoidably he sinks into those beautiful years after the liberation: enchanting Italy, before Rosa, before the children. If it hadn't been for that mistake, he would be sitting in the Saint George Islands now, those marvelous islands, unpopulated, shedding silence and water all day and all night. A mistake will always be a mistake, and that's what made him roll from place to place. Now he is here, in Jaffa. The girls have grown up and come to look like their mother. They have inherited her facial expressions too. He had made a big effort to cut himself off from them. Now he might sit for two hours without having their shadow pass before his eyes. Now they belonged to the hidden regions of his life.

At around ten the first traders enter the café. They know Bartfuss well, from Italy. Usually they aren't at ease with men like Bartfuss. They're suspicious of men who don't talk a lot. But they don't boycott Bartfuss, because he's a legend. They were in the camps too, but not in the same camp, from which only faint echoes had come. So even though he doesn't tell them anything, they know: everything he went through is true and certain. If he were to sit there and reveal even a handbreadth they would thank him, but Bartfuss won't utter a word. They could easily boycott him, and a lot of actions could be chalked up against him, but still they don't boycott him. Bartfuss, for his part, never did anything to make them like him. On the contrary, everything he did was to his discredit.

At around ten the whole place fills up with dealers. Bartfuss goes out. For a long time he wanders along the shore. The sea and the cigarettes inebriate him again. He eats lunch in Tina's restaurant. When he was in Italy steak joints already disgusted him. But Tina's place has a kind of tranquility you can apparently find only in cellars. Here no one asks who you are and what you're doing. Cool darkness envelops everyone. She serves Bartfuss a cheese omelet and cold borscht. Here he sometimes sits until as late as three.

Immediately after leaving the restaurant he turns down a side street and heads for the two-story house. When he gets close to the building his gait changes. His back bends, his steps lengthen, and he hugs the wall. That walk lasts only a few moments. When he's inside, in the narrow room, he shades his eyes for a moment. Now he knows what he has to do. He buys and sells. He doesn't bargain. Here his movements are sharp, quick, and precise. He adds the numbers in his head. The whole thing lasts no more than a quarter of an hour.

At the door he lights a cigarette and, with quick steps, he heads toward the sea. That short period of concentration has left him limp. Formerly those deals would disturb him afterward too. Now he doesn't think about them, only at night sometimes, on his bed, but not excessively.

At that hour the street is full of dealers and agents. Their grimaces and haste revolt him. Especially the religious ones. A few years ago he had stood here and shouted loudly at them: "Why don't you play some sports? Why don't you go swimming? You make the seashore ugly." That was just an outburst. Now a scab has also formed over that revulsion. Except for the smells of kerosene and oil he would even have lingered to observe them.

On warm, humid evenings he gets on a bus and goes out of town, as far as Natanya. The darkness and the pitching motion of the bus gently soothe his overwrought senses. He gulps down a bottle of beer, and the feeling of loneliness is blurred. A year ago a woman had accosted him, and he had spent the whole night with her. In the morning he had gone back all muddled and fallen asleep in the café. Now he won't allow himself any adventures like that. He would rather wander along the shore or cruise in a bus. The movement intoxicates him.

Occasionally Rosa still dares to break in—money, of course. She's ten years younger than he. You can't see it on her now. She's gotten fat, and an unpleasant grayness has settled at the roots of her hair. She doesn't work. Most of the day she lolls on pillows, drinks tea, and eats sandwiches. Once her outbursts used to fill his entire day with noise. Now he has learned to ignore them, not to answer her. He leaves a sum of money on the table and goes out without saying anything. But sometimes the married daughter bursts in with her mother's noise and lays down masses of words. That pains him to this day.

When he returns late at night they're immersed in sleep. He goes inside to his room and immediately closes the door after him. As he takes his shoes off he notices that a few more strips of light lie on the floor, because the shutter has cracked and split in the summer. That discovery doesn't please him terribly. Except for the women, he would get up and drink a glass of lemon soda. There was lemon soda in the refrigerator, but that would mean opening the door. She might ask in her sleep: "Who's there?" He stretches out on the bed. And when it seems to him that she's listening, he wraps himself in the blanket.

That's how it's been for years, day after day, at an ever-faster pace, but without any great changes.

2

 TRUE, THERE HAD also been other days, when they spoke. They had been so few and so short that nothing remained of them except a kind of distant twilight. The barren silence that had overrun them had left nothing of those days, not even a scrap. Even in their second year together the sentences were truncated and had come out as mumbles, actually kinds of syllables that had quickly become like thorns. And since then:

"Did you leave any?"

"What?"

"What I asked for."

"I don't remember."

"Remember."

"What?"

"I told you: money for the grocery store."

In the end he would give it to her and go out. The open spaces, the deals, would make him forget her, and only upon his return would he wrap himself in silence. As though it weren't his house but rather a treacherous area of life, where you had to avoid giving away too much. In time he was sorry that in moments of bodily intimacy he had told her a few secrets.

For her part, to tell the truth, she had tried. Once she had even let out a cry of despair: "Let's talk." Those attempts closed him off even more, but his attention wasn't at all impaired. Over the years he had learned to interpret every one of her movements, every twist of her mouth, before a word left her throat.

But she insisted: the girls. She didn't educate them. She kneaded them in her hands like soft dough. From day to day they took on more of their mother's look. Mostly Bridget. Her blurred, damaged face absorbed all her mother's grimaces without any selection. For some reason he was sorrier about Bridget. He had some hidden regard for her. Maybe because of her smile, which spread out sometimes in a kind of mute agreement with him.

That was only an appearance. Bridget clung to her mother with anxious rigidity.

About the past, of course, they never spoke. But the past would pop up at moments when it wasn't expected at all. The thought that all during the war she had been in a village with peasants, sleeping with the old man and his sons by turns, that thought wouldn't loose its grip on him even in the bluntest moments of oblivion. There had been times when the thought would pop up every day: Rosa learned to slip away from that area with agility, like an animal. But in fact she didn't try to deny the accusation, and sometimes it even seemed she was thinking about those days with pleasure.

Occasionally he would hear her say, "This is how they

fix beets in the village," or, "This bread tastes of the oven." While the girls were still children he would hear her telling them about life in the village, about fruit picking and harvests. She told it without any grace, but still he imagined he heard longing in her voice.

Sometimes he couldn't stand it anymore, and he'd break in: "Life isn't everything. There's a limit to humiliation."

Apparently she understood the meaning of those sentences and wouldn't respond. But concerning the house, the girls, she stood her own ground and made strong demands.

So the wall became more solid. When the girls were children and Rosa wasn't at home, he would exchange a few sentences with them. Those few sentences taught him how deeply they were immersed in their mother's life. They used to call him "him." "He" was a stranger of whom one had to be wary.

For his part he also tried to plant a few grains of poison in the girls' souls, but they were so reserved and cautious with him that they didn't register the words he spoke. Not even the boxes of candy helped. They were her faithful cubs.

Paula went to school at the right age. Her report cards satisfied her mother. They didn't show him the reports. That area was closed to him. He often tried to find the report cards. They were well hidden. Bridget didn't go to school. Rosa shielded her beneath her two solid wings. Several times the question of an institution for retarded children came up. Rosa rejected every proposal. She believed she alone had the power to cure the girl. Within herself, after Paula had grown up, she would accuse him, for a father's rejection is an infectious disease. Who, if not he, had brought that disease? Whenever she found a character trait in the girl that displeased her, she would attribute it to him: an irresponsible father, estranged, full of evil filth.

She was sure that at night he sowed his wicked thoughts in Bridget's sleep. The fact was the girl woke up sometimes; she wasn't focused, and she got mixed up whenever he was spoken of.

Sometimes he was surprised by the warmth he felt for Bridget. On days when fire burst out at home and scraps of words flew about in the air, Bridget wouldn't take part in the quarrel. She would curl up in a corner, making Rosa furious. Sometimes Rosa would tell her, "Go to him. You're like him." That sentence, which she rarely pronounced, caused him pleasure, like a hidden pain.

But more than anything he distanced himself from them. He put a lot of effort into distancing himself from them. He often thought of leaving Israel and going back to Italy. He didn't do it because he didn't want to grant her a permanent excuse: because of him. She used to cherish that phrase with malice. Maybe he also harbored a secret hope that the girls might return to him.

The girls didn't return. From year to year the distance seemed to expand. He would watch them grow from a distance, wild growth. Rosa, for her part, worked unstintingly. She sent Paula to French lessons. Paula would come back from those evening lessons full of enthusiasm. Older boys were studying with her. Rosa didn't abandon Bridget for even an hour. Until Bridget was ten Rosa fed her her meals. She emptied her whole self into Bridget's soul, even a few words of Polish.

She would always surprise him: "Give."

"I don't have anything."

"What, again you don't have anything?"

"Not now. I'll give you something later."

"You hear, girls." She would immediately mobilize her silent advocates. While they were still children she shared all her grievances with them. In time she sent Paula to wrangle with him.

Thus the wall grew more solid. Nevertheless not a sound failed to reach him, the throbbing of their sleep and their whispers, and of course their laughter and coughing.

3

 SOMETIMES HE WOULD hear Rosa: "He gets up early. He always gets up at the same time." There was no praise in her voice, only a hint of warning. She observed his ways closely, all her senses alert.

Once she said, "He's always awake."

There was some truth to that claim. He never let himself sleep deeply. Over the years his body had acquired a few little warning buzzers that woke him whenever deep sleep was about to overcome him. For her part Rosa developed a special vocabulary for him. His way of walking, his way of eating. But she was especially aware of his sleep. "He doesn't sleep, he just dozes. Even in the winter he doesn't sleep." Remarks like that sharpened his alertness even more, heightening his wakefulness. That wakefulness protected him even when he would come back from long trips, tired and nearly fainting.

Sometimes sleep would seize him in an unexpected place, sitting or even standing. Not for hours. He would

rouse himself quickly, clear away the cobwebs, and recover. Those catnaps made him restive. He was wary of
them, or rather, he kept reminding himself to be mindful
of them.

More than anyone he was cautious with Rosa. Rosa
knew he was secretly fostering his alertness, and so she
would warn herself: He also listens from a distance. Once
she told Bridget: "Close the door, I can't stand it when
people eavesdrop." She, of course, meant him. He wasn't
in his room at the time. She was sure he was trying to
confuse her. He did nothing that could be construed as
intervention. On the contrary, he hardly spoke, as little
as he could. If he had to answer, he would answer with
a single word, or no more than two. Over the years he
developed a clipped language of refusal, protective syllables that were accompanied with a shrug of his left shoul-
der, all of which said, "Leave me alone."

Rosa kept a few words to herself, which she called
promises, and she would repeat them in tired phrases:
"Where are the promises? Where are the beautiful
words?" She referred to the first days, when they still
spoke. Now she would lay down those words like stones.

He had met Rosa on the shore in Italy, among the
many refugees, bewildered people, between the shacks
and the water. That summer overcame everyone, confused everyone, addled people's brains and made them
blunt, clumsy, and hungry for the sun.

As noted, he met Rosa on the beach. He said, "Come,"
and she got up and followed him. It was the same the next
day. She didn't ask questions. Her body was full and
young and smelled of the sea and cheap cologne.

She didn't say, "Do you love me?" or, "When will you come back?" She didn't even ask his name. The coastal sun ruled over everyone and enveloped them like sleep. Everything transpired as if under a heavy glass bell. It was a wakeful sleep but full of suction. Once he found her sitting and eating sardines. "You want to eat?" she held out the can.

"I'm full."

"In that case I'm throwing this into the sea," she said and threw it.

There was strength in her arm as she swung it.

They would make love for an hour or two. Afterward he would part from her without even leaving her a single word. An hour of lovemaking would make her sleepy. After a while he noticed that her expression was serene. When he first brought her a box of candy she took it and said, "This is good." Without offering him any she ate it. He asked her if it was sweet and she said, "It's very sweet."

She would sit by the sea for hours. He knew that he would always find her by the sea.

Once he asked, for some reason, "How did you get here?" He meant to ask, "How did you survive?" She answered simply, "I was with peasants."

"And so you were saved."

"The peasants dressed me in their clothes."

"You felt good?"

"I worked."

"The peasants where you worked demanded favors from you?"

"Not a lot," she said, smiling.

He didn't ask any more, and she didn't tell.

It was a summer full of light, full of power. People labored like ants. At the end of the day sleep would prostrate them where they stood. Bartfuss was like the rest. He bought, sold, and smuggled, and in the evening he would come to Rosa. Rosa didn't ask, "Who are you and what do you do?" Other women would scream and shake the world. Rosa wasn't a bother. She knew that at night he would find her by the sea.

"You don't ask anything." He would sometimes surprise her.

"What's to ask?"

"Just the same."

Once he went as far as the Saint George Islands with the fishermen. He was there for a week. He was sure that upon his return he wouldn't find her anymore. To his surprise she was there, and to his surprise she didn't ask, "Where were you?" Her silence charmed him.

But he was curious and wanted to know more. For example, how many peasants were there in that village? Did she go out to the meadows? Where did they lodge her in the winter? Her answer was short: "I didn't do anything special." "She's smart," he said to himself.

It went on that way. Autumn came with winds and frost. Not far from the shore Rosa found an abandoned shed and squatted in it. She didn't have a lot of possessions, and the few she had satisfied her needs. That autumn she told him some details about herself, not of her own free will, but because he pressed her.

She was the only daughter from a traditional home in a small city. At home they read newspapers and books. In the city there was no high school, so her parents sent her to the one in the district capital, where she studied for two years. What interested her? Geography. When the war broke out she was seventeen. She was separated from her parents, and ran away to the village. In the village a peasant couple adopted her, old friends of her father's. She stayed in the village for three years. She told her story, not all at once, but in answer to explicit questions. One evening she told him, "I think I'm pregnant." He was surprised, and in his panic he spat out a few angry words. Rosa burst into tears. He didn't try to console her.

Many evil thoughts had teemed in his brain then. For example: pay her off, abandon her, and flee to Palestine. She, to his surprise, didn't plead with him. Her movements changed little, and her body broadened. Her eyes were full of heavy wonderment. In time he noticed that the shed had also changed. She had hung a few small carpets on the wall. Even a picture cut out of a magazine. He didn't ask about her future. He came and sat by her side, without hugging her.

At that time he was a partner in a big ring, the Ungar Ring, which was active along the Italian coast. Ungar, the man who founded it, died of a stroke and didn't live to see its expansion. The ring did a lot of amazing things. Some people say that between one smuggling operation and another they also organized illegal immigration to Palestine. Among the smugglers were a few high school teachers. Bartfuss got so involved in his business that he lost sight of Rosa's pregnancy. But Rosa didn't disappear. Her body got fuller from day to day. Her thin features were erased, and she got fat.

"If I go, what will you do?" She didn't seem concerned about his intentions. That was both her strength and her charm. He could have left her. Many women were abandoned. Every man for himself. That was the way of life and the line of thought. For some reason he didn't do it. In fact he fled from any decision.

Meanwhile her pregnancy advanced. Her fine, contained movements were lost. She had to support herself with both hands when she sat down.

He got angry: how had she managed to bamboozle him? He asked her directly, "Why didn't you tell me earlier?"

"What?"

"That you were pregnant."

"I told you."

A great many suspicions teemed in his brain. A woman sits on the seaside and anyone who wants her takes her. A woman wouldn't refuse a bed for the night. The peasants in the village slept with her too. The thought that the peasants in the village had also slept with her wouldn't leave him even when he was traveling, intoxicated with his huge smuggling operations.

"I'll never see her face again. In fact, she doesn't care. Women like Rosa raise their children in the sand." But in spite of himself, he would go back; not only that, but he would sit with her a lot.

The peasants again. "Why did you sleep with the peasants, just to survive? There's a limit to disgrace. Life is valuable, but not at any price." She apparently understood his arguments and kept silent.

"So, you agree."

He tortured her like that. She learned to hear and not answer. He would sit for hours and stare at her. She wasn't pretty, and now that she was pregnant she was even awkward, but there was some power in her being, an incomprehensible power.

Around then the matter of illegal immigration arose. He would dispatch illegal immigrants and smuggle at the same time. The trips were very dangerous, but danger was his element. He lived for the strong taste of action on others' behalf, like in the forest. The issue of Palestine didn't concern him, but yearning for it strengthened him.

Meanwhile the older girl was born. He wasn't there for the birth. Upon his return he found an infant screaming at Rosa's breast. She called her Paula, and he asked why. Later he found out it was the name of a popular singer. That irritated him, but he didn't say anything.

Right after Paula's birth a kind of change took place in Rosa's face. The muscles of her chin grew stronger. He was sure it was a temporary change, but he was mistaken: with Paula's birth her self-assurance increased. "The baby needs to sleep. Why didn't you bring apples from the country?" Whereas other women complained, shouted abuse, and lost their wits, Rosa's body got more solid.

More than once he was about to leave the camp and sail away. Boats were sailing to Australia, Brazil, and New Zealand. Many husbands left their wives and sailed away. Separation was easier to understand than attachment. But he, for some reason, would go back to her like a criminal returning to the scene of the crime.

They would fight until late at night. She didn't lack for words now. She made use of the words she had learned in the village. She said: "I have no claims against you."

Or sometimes, "Men will always be men." Once she even said, "I won't bring you to court. The Joint will provide for me," meaning the Jewish Joint Distribution Committee. That sentence made him angrier than all the other things she said. He persisted: "Life is valuable, but there's a limit to disgrace." Actually he was the one talking in the wrong context. It had taken him a while to sense a kind of impurity in his life. Where that impurity was, he still didn't know. In the midst of everything the child got sick.

There was no doctor there, and he rushed off to bring one from Naples. The doctor diagnosed dysentery. Rosa paled at the bad news. For several days the baby fought with the Angel of Death. Rosa didn't let her out of her hands even for a moment.

While Rosa was battling the Angel of Death, he was climbing in the mountains, bringing goods across and dragging elderly immigrants. Rosa completely faded out of his mind. The baby's illness filled it. He saw the baby in many different ways at that time. Annoyingly he remembered the picture of an anguished madonna hanging at the entrance to the church with a baby at her breast. The struggle lasted for two weeks. One morning the child woke with a healthy face. Rosa's happiness was boundless. Bartfuss too breathed easily.

In those feverish days his language began to take shape, a language with no words, a language that was all eavesdropping, alert senses, and impressions. Even then he learned to mute every sensation. But more than that, he stopped thinking. The bare mountains would soak the thoughts out of him. He would come home weary, exhausted, and collapse like a sack.

While he was still in doubt, involved in hectic activity,

learning to repress his anger, Rosa announced that she was pregnant again. The news stunned him. He was boiling, but not a word left his mouth. At night he got drunk, and in the morning when he arose from his drunkenness, the thought flashed within him that all the things that were happening to him weren't things that he wanted to have happen. Maybe Rosa was subject to the same vain enchantment.

After Bridget's birth Rosa's body got fatter and fatter. Her face took on a kind of annoying serenity. She didn't want to go to Palestine. Once she said to herself: "We'll be among Jews again."

The girls grew. Their growth didn't arouse any interest in him. He had his own secrets, which he was developing assiduously: coffee in the morning, the sea, every once in a while an abandoned woman. Secretly he hoped the days would have action in store for him, sacrifice, some plunge that would purify his body. Mighty deeds didn't happen along so quickly.

While he was fleeing and returning, a few members of the great Ungar Ring were caught. He had to run away. First he thought of running to Brazil, but at that time no ship was sailing to Brazil. Having no choice he joined the illegal immigrants. For a week he was jostled among the illegal immigrants on the coast. Finally he pushed his way into a small ship that was waiting for them at an abandoned pier. It was cold, and for a few days he didn't pick his head up out of his blanket. When he opened his eyes he saw she was there, with the two girls at her bosom.

4

 SHE NEVER FORGAVE him for running away. She told the girls again and again that in Italy their father had already tried to run away, but that she, with her great presence of mind, had thwarted his evil design. She used a special tone of voice when she spoke about that victory.

At those moments his hatred seethed, and he could have hit her—something he had never done, of course. But in recent years that argument had provoked a different reaction in him, you might say a different hatred: he would stare at her with a kind of quiet look that drove her mad. She couldn't stand those looks and would rush to mobilize her cubs. "Look at the way he's looking at me. What did I do to him to have him look at me that way? Let him confess once and for all. Let his daughters know." That look, that venom, were his strength then. She kept on: "He tried to run away. I'll never forget that."

Rosa had many different faces at that time, but she was

never alone. Her two cubs sprawled on her and she showered them with affection. Even the weak Bridget, that groggy girl, was on her side. Privately he had to admit that she was a mother after all. But their joy would make him so angry that it hurt.

Rosa knew what she was doing. Over the years the three of them became a single mass. They ate together and slept together. And they had their own language: "This is nice and this isn't nice," leafing through the same magazine. The time of Paula's engagement was festive. Of course they didn't include him. It can't be said that this didn't annoy him. After Paula's wedding Bridget belonged entirely to Rosa. She fed her and dressed her and put jewels around her neck. In the summer they went to the beach together. Rosa believed that the sea salt would cure the girl. They would spend many hours together in the sea. On their return from the sea they would loll about and slurp down ice cream. And the sea did leave its mark on Bridget. She grew broader and her full face expressed a kind of satisfaction. Except for some tics she had the look of a buxom young girl. Her teeth were white and strong too.

In the winter they sat in the double bed a lot. In the winter Bridget's questions had a kind of transparent clarity: Why didn't they send her to school like Paula? Why did boys pester her? Rosa would explain to her, and Bridget would laugh. For hours they would sit and laugh.

He, of course, was not forgotten in those conversations. He was the dark shadow, the unsolved riddle. Sometimes he would find Bridget at the threshold. "What are you doing?" Rosa would come right out and drive her back into the house. Those doorstep meetings were rare and short, but they would leave a kind of shame and revulsion in him. Within himself he had to admit: Bridget wasn't a stranger to him. Rosa was aware of that hidden affinity and stayed on guard. No contact and no speech. So things went, year after year, until March.

5

 On march 17, which was no different from other days, he came home sooner than usual. He meant to do some figures. Gold had gone way up, and that rise also thrilled him. The dealers, who just a few days ago had been running away from gold, now looked panicked in the streets, drugged, gripped by fear. Bartfuss had done the impossible again, and their eyes were shot through with jealousy. While he was sitting and adding up the figures on little pieces of cardboard, a kind of blunt pain passed through his upper abdomen, near his chest, and then it immediately loosed its grip.

Later the pain came back again, but this time without remission. "It hurts." A sound escaped his throat. Yanked from her sleep, Rosa appeared. "Did you call me?" She burst in. But seeing him collapsed next to the bed she settled down and she said, "You're sick. I'll get a doctor right away."

The old doctor arrived at once, wide awake, with his

doctor's kit. He leaned over and felt the sick man's hand. His movements showed great patience. He immediately declared that Bartfuss would have to be taken to the hospital. Bridget had also woken up. She stood in the doorway and her staring eyes expressed the numbness of someone who has been roused out of sleep.

"What is it?" asked Rosa.

"A slight attack, probably an ulcer. What has he been doing in the past few days?"

"Same as usual."

"How old is he?"

"Fifty."

"Does he smoke, or drink?"

"Moderately."

"What does he do?"

"He's a trader."

It had been years since he heard her speaking directly about him. The short questions and answers sliced into his muffled consciousness in flashes. The doctor's cold hands, which had not ceased probing him, felt pleasant. It seemed to him as though somebody else, also a stranger, was observing the doctor's movements.

"What did he eat for supper?" asked the doctor.

"I didn't see. He came home late."

Now it seemed as if the doctor were about to lean over and ask him a discrete question. He didn't. He went down to his knees and leaned over the patient with cautious movements and straightened out his body. Rosa rushed to fetch a pillow from the cupboard.

"Mother," asked Bridget, "what happened?"

"Can't you see?" Rosa scolded her.

Bridget withdrew in alarm.

About an hour later the ambulance came. Rosa put on her long, flowery dress. Her full face was wide awake now. The old doctor had already managed to pack up his instruments, and handed her a slip of paper. The young stretcher-bearers did their work quickly. The transfer was smooth.

Bartfuss opened his eyes. Now he didn't feel pain anymore. A kind of relieved weakness spread across his body. The emergency room was full. No escorts were allowed in. People stood indolently by the barred windows, as if in a cage. A powerful fan hummed on the ceiling.

He was awake. The thin joy that had made him happy a moment before the attack seemed to come back to him. He was also pleased he had managed to conceal the gold in its hiding place. He had no doubt that when she went back home she would immediately hurry over and poke around inside the cupboard, the mattress, and his pockets. Her disappointment would be bitter: not a single penny.

He had built the hiding place with his own hands, in the cellar; it was a deep hiding place, where no one would suspect it, well camouflaged, dry, and, at certain hours, accessible. The thought that they were now going through the cupboard, shaking blankets, gnashing teeth, secretly gave pleasure to his weakness.

Toward morning Rosa came in. Her fallen face expressed a kind of gray worry. It seemed to him that she was about to ask him to reveal, if only for the children's sake, the location of the hiding place. That was just a mistaken feeling. She asked him how he was.

"Better."

"What did the doctors do to you?"

"Nothing."

"They didn't ask?"

"No."

Her dry, emotionless face suddenly filled with suspicion. He knew that face well.

"What about Bridget?" he asked, for some reason.

"She's at home."

It had been a long time since he'd spoken Bridget's name. Bridget had been born two and a half years after the liberation. Rosa had insisted that they call the girl Bridget. That was her dream, she said. As a matter of fact the subject wasn't at all important to him. Very few children were born on that open coast. Strange names were given to them, like Margaretta and Tolpina.

Rosa's closeness, after years of estrangement, didn't move him. Now he could look closely at the flushed patches across her neck, at the gold pendant, her full hands crossed in front of her. Now suspicion was garbed in cold moderation on her face.

"I feel better." He tried to free her of this obligation.

"What did they say to you? Didn't they give you any medicine?"

"I told you," he said curtly.

There was nothing left for her to do but survey the room and the two patients lying pale next to him. Compared to them Bartfuss looked healthy.

"Don't they give you blankets here?" she asked, aggrieved.

Bartfuss didn't answer. He expected her to ask for money now. He was curious as to how she would do it.

"I'm going. I'll be back," she said, and turned to the door.

She'll do it later, he thought to himself.

By noon his weakness had passed, and he ate with a hearty appetite. Now Paula appeared before his eyes. As a baby she had been thin and weak. Milk hadn't nourished her. After months of struggle she overcame her weakness and started growing. Rosa attributed it to the fresh apples she bought from the peasants in the village.

He was involved in big smuggling operations, spread over southern Italy. That activity intoxicated him.

Even then he had spoken little to her. The coastal sun had turned her brown. When he came home from his trips he would collapse, thirsty for sleep.

"What are you doing? What are you smuggling?"

"Why do you have to know?"

From day to day his trade expanded and grew riskier. His face was gradually covered with a different kind of swarthiness, the swarthiness of secrecy. The third year of their stay in Italy they began to be squeezed in a vise. Some people were caught, others managed to get away to Sicily. One evening he said to her: "Things aren't good."

"What's wrong with here?"

"Nothing's wrong, but it's dangerous."

She apparently didn't understand the intricacies. He also didn't bother explaining them to her.

In time she attributed all her troubles to their escape. In Israel he cut himself off from the rings, but he didn't stop trading. In fact, because of his trade he grew more introverted and friendless. His love for Rosa was extinguished by itself. Hostility secretly sprouted up, from sentence to sentence.

Rosa clung to the girls with obstinate diligence. They became like her, and not only in their looks. When they grew older she also got them to love the color of her dresses. At eighteen the elder one married a short, solidly built young man, born in some neglected farm town. Bartfuss exchanged a few sentences with him and nothing more. There was something noisy about the way he talked. Rosa saw the marriage as a success. The daughter went to live on her husband's farm.

The next morning Rosa came to visit with Bridget. They were wearing bright, flowery dresses. Bridget stood behind her mother's back as though afraid to be seen.

"How are you feeling?" asked Rosa.

"Good."

"What did the doctors say?"

"Good."

Rosa surveyed the length of the room. Her face expressed dissatisfaction. Bridget stood clumsily behind her mother.

"Didn't they say anything to you?" She kneaded her words again. "I brought you fruit."

"Why?"

"They certainly don't give you fruit here."

"They do, plenty."

"I know them," she said in a heavily feminine tone.

"I won't argue with you," he said for some reason.

"I'm sure you're right." She pulled out that worn old sentence for him, which she hadn't used for years. The words brought a weak smile to his lips.

Her chin dropped and suspicion filled her face. Now her eyes probed every corner of the room. She seemed to be collecting evidence to prove how neglected the place was. She wiped her forehead with her handkerchief and the medallion trembled on her heaving chest.

In Italy he had bought that medallion from a refugee on his way to Australia. A distant relative had sent the refugee a boat ticket, but he hadn't sent money. The medallion was his last souvenir of home, and he was willing to sell it on one weak condition: that if he ever prospered, he would have the right to buy it back at its full value. Bartfuss refused to swear, but he promised him with a handshake. The refugee knew it was a feeble promise, but he apparently needed the promise at that moment. The deal was concluded.

The refugee sailed to Australia. Sometimes Bartfuss dreamt about him at night. One day he managed to find the refugee's address, and he wrote him a long, detailed letter. No answer came. From time to time, over the years, he thought about that anonymous refugee and the weak promise he had given him. Rosa adopted the medallion with ease and hung it around her neck. After a while he told her he felt like returning the medallion to its owner. Rosa's answer was simple: "Don't be too righteous. It doesn't become you."

"It disturbs me," he once complained.

"That disturbs you, and other things don't disturb you."

He also stopped talking about that.

Now it was time to part. The nurse on duty pressed the visitors to leave. Rosa said, "I'm going. I'll be here tomorrow."

"Don't take too much trouble."

"You're sick. I won't argue with you," she said, and

turned her head toward the door. Bridget stepped aside. In profile she was an exact copy of her mother. Rosa put out her hand as one does to a little child. Bridget responded and reached her hand out to her. They left.

The doctors were pleased. The examinations showed an improvement. Except for the thought that Rosa would come in the afternoon, he would even have enjoyed his forced seclusion. His neighbor in the room had also improved. Between one meal and another they played chess.

One evening a patient approached him and said, "Your face looks familiar to me."

"My name is Bartfuss," said Bartfuss.

"Wait a moment. It's you. If I'm not mistaken, they tell amazing stories about you."

"About me?"

"Your name is Bartfuss, right? Then . . ."

Bartfuss tried to evade the patient's glance, but the patient wouldn't let up: "Tell me," his eyes begged.

"What is there to tell?" Bartfuss's voice trembled.

"Every word is precious to me."

"There's nothing to tell. You yourself know."

"But they tell astounding things about you."

"Why are you doing this to me?"

"Just tell me one thing, and I'll be grateful for the rest of my life."

"What?"

"Let me touch you," the patient said, surprisingly, and put out his hand.

Bartfuss wanted to strike that thin, outstretched hand, but he didn't. He turned aside and escaped into the bathroom.

The next day Rosa surprised him: she came with the married daughter, Paula. Since the wedding he hadn't seen her. Her face had grown darker and her body was that of a mature woman.

"How are you?" she asked without standing on ceremony.

"Good."

"You look fine, what are you doing here?"

Bartfuss didn't answer. He sucked his lower lip into his mouth and looked as if he were trying to find a word.

His daughter went on: "Mother is worried."

"It doesn't depend on me," said Bartfuss.

"A lot does depend on your wishes."

Bartfuss didn't respond.

Bitter arguments had been held in the house for whole months before Paula's wedding. Bartfuss set aside a certain sum. The mother and daughter found that sum inadequate and shameful. Bartfuss, for his part, claimed he didn't have any more. Because of that argument he hadn't come to the ceremony. They had held it at the farm. He occasionally saw Paula's husband from a distance in Jaffa. The boy didn't appeal to him.

During the fight certain words popped up that hadn't found release before that. Money, of course. "Where is the money?" Bartfuss denied that he had hidden supplies of money. It was a game of hide-and-seek. They all knew the truth, at least they imagined they did. Rosa had instructed the girls that their father had a lot of money, hidden away, that he kept from them. The girls grew up on that legend.

"You look well," Paula repeated. That superficial remark pleased him, but he immediately recovered his wits and realized that it wasn't as innocent as it sounded. It's better to have him live. As long as we don't know the location of his hiding place, it's better to have him live. He understood that, and his hidden anger rose up within him. But Paula was cunning and disguised her intentions. She told him about the farm, about her two-year-old son.

Bartfuss didn't ask. It was better not to ask. You might get entangled, leave yourself open, and show something you hadn't intended to reveal. Now he felt she had inherited some of his own cunning. For a moment that little discovery pleased him, but he immediately commanded himself to act with restraint.

Paula told him without overdoing it. That too, it seemed, she had learned from him. Rosa stood at her side, and the whole time her eyes followed the events in the room. Clearly she didn't intend to mix in, except for a word here and there, to show she was listening.

"I'm going home," said Paula.

Rosa straightened her dress and took a small bundle of fruit from her handbag; without asking his permission she put it on his bedside table.

"What's that?" Bartfuss was startled.

"Fruit."

Money wasn't discussed this time either. Bartfuss knew that if it weren't for the money they probably wouldn't have come. He felt a kind of thin pleasure from their need for him. Now they would come every day.

As his health improved he understood that life without coffee and cigarettes would be flat and stale. Without being aware of it, and without wanting to, he started thinking. He had invested a lot of energy into blocking up the openings through which thoughts could push out. In recent years he had managed to seal them off almost completely. Now he felt he didn't have the power to stop them anymore. Again Italy, again the Rosa before Rosa. In Italy no one got married. It was a crossroads where people loved, smuggled, and gobbled down food. No one knew what to do with the lives that had been saved. The lives that had been saved strove for great deeds.

By and by he recovered. Now he had to rest at home for a while. It had been a mild attack, in the end, hardly an attack at all, the doctor joked, but he should still rest. In the afternoon he returned home.

Rosa was surprised and said, "They let you go?"

"As you see."

His room was open and two illustrated magazines were on his bed, a sign that someone had been lying there.

"Who's been lying in my bed?" The words burst out against his will.

"Shuki, your son-in-law," she said.

He noticed that another chair had been brought in, a sign that besides him there had been someone else. The smell of cigarette smoke hung in the air. Now he had no doubt that they had picked up the floor tiles and poked around. The thought that for days they had worked at pulling them up secretly pleased him, but he didn't hold his tongue. He asked, "What have you been doing in here?"

"I don't understand."

"I'm asking you."

"Nothing, don't you see?"

He opened the cupboard. Here too were signs of the probing hands. He didn't ask again.

Rosa stood there. Her silent presence merely reinforced his suspicions. They had poked around. A few years ago the nest egg had been hidden under a floor tile, but one day he began to suspect that Rosa might break down the door. Now, of course, she hadn't missed the opportunity. Rosa withdrew, and he closed the door behind her. He lay down on the bed and listened. The familiar voices, the many whispers, filtered in to him clearly.

"He's back," she announced.

"What's he doing?" asked Bridget.

"You're asking me?"

"How does he look?"

"No change."

They spoke about him with exaggerated use of the third person. Bartfuss knew the ins and outs of that way of talking. But now it seemed to him that in his absence it had been perfected, stripped of all sentiment.

Still his pleasure returned. I'm alive. The modicum of his egotism, which he had never dared to release, throbbed in him like fanfares of victory. Now he expected that the murmurings would die down, and when they did, he would set out.

Outside, the evening twilight had already come. There was some celebration in the street. Everyone streamed toward the seashore. "Where are you going?" He wanted to address them as old friends. He had no acquaintances. Everyone was sunk in his own walk.

Tina asked, "Where have you been? We haven't seen

you for ages." Bartfuss noticed she said, "We haven't seen you," the plural, a sign that the other customers had also noticed his absence. The words pleased him this time. Tina was a simple woman, as simple as they come. Years of suffering were visible in every one of her movements. As though she weren't the owner but a modest waitress, concerned not only with people's honor but also with their hidden feelings. Her food also had a kind of modesty. A quiet pleasure washed over him. Later too, when he stood in the street, which had emptied by now, the pleasure did not leave him. "I'm alive again."

He met Dorf in a café. For years he hadn't seen him. He too had been in one of the smaller camps, near the notorious S. camp. He too had survived—in a strange way, in fact. They had taken him out of the camp and shot him, shot him many times, but none of the bullets had struck a vital organ. Another miracle: one of the other men who had been shot, a companion in forced labor, had a few slices of bread in his pocket and a bottle of water. The small quantity of bread and the water nourished Dorf for a few days, and apparently also helped him recover, because after that he crawled several kilometers until he reached the forest. In the forest the bread also nourished him. And when Bartfuss reached the forest Dorf was already healthy, optimistic, ready to live again.

They spent several months in the forest, living in a foxhole they had dug with their bare fingers. The retreating Germans dragged their equipment along the road, and defeat was heard in every creaking wheel. The prolonged downfall of the Germans restored their faith in life.

At the end of the war they parted easily, like a package coming apart by itself. Later he saw Dorf in Naples and ignored him. Now Dorf addressed him softly, as one addresses a brother. Bartfuss was mute with embarrassment and called out: "Forgive me. I didn't recognize you. It's been years since we've seen each other. What kind of work are you doing now? Are you happy?"

"I work in the port. And you?"

"Nothing."

"You mean, business."

"Not exactly." A strange smile spread on Bartfuss's face.

"You mean to say you're not involved, how shall I say it . . ."

"No."

"Then show me your hands."

Now Bartfuss felt that his former friend, whom he had ignored for years, was trying to make him feel distressed. He put out his two white hands.

"Those two hands haven't worked for years," Dorf declared.

"What do you want from me?" Bartfuss tried to shake him off.

"Nothing. For my part you can do whatever you want. I won't inform on you."

"What do you mean?" For some reason Bartfuss raised his voice.

"I don't know how to explain it to you. You'll certainly understand. Words don't come easily to me. But you'll understand."

"Of course." Bartfuss accommodated him.

"You can deal in whatever you want. I won't inform on you. But why here? Why pollute this place?"

"Now I understand," said Bartfuss and rose to his feet.

"That's all I wanted to say to you."

"Now I understand," Bartfuss repeated, and turned away. Dorf didn't follow him. Afterward Bartfuss walked along the dark shore. The salty humidity dissolved his emotions. He was no longer angry. A strange kind of staleness gnawed at his soul. He knew: the words that had come out of Dorf's mouth weren't Dorf's words, but words he had absorbed at some meeting, maybe someone had whispered them in his ear. Dorf didn't know clichés. They had been together for many days, and he had never used clichés. More than the insult, Dorf's strange use of clichés pained him, but as he walked he became more certain that the Dorf who had accosted him wasn't Dorf. Dorf had died in the forest. The one wandering around was only an evil spirit.

6

Now THEY WERE ALL thinking about his illness, as though a new region of hope had been opened before them. It was a peculiar combination of greed, cunning, and hopefulness, but, more than anything, eavesdropping: what is he doing and what is he going to do? In fact they sat and ate, for hours they sat and ate, as if to prolong the life of that hope as much as possible. Rosa would cook summery dishes, what the peasants called "raw soups." As she did so she told them about the ways of the village, about sowing and reaping. She had a lot of words. The son-in-law was amused. He would voice extravagant praise and tease his wife.

Rosa's face was strange then. On her forehead was a mixture of sadness and malicious joy. She would talk about her bad years as though everything were behind her. Paula and her husband were alarmingly practical. They didn't believe their eyes. As long as Bartfuss was coming and going there was no sense in talking about great expectations. Rosa, despite everything, had some relation with the occult. She believed that the wheel of fortune was about to favor her again.

Bridget would ask an occasional question, but her questions were paid no attention. Rosa would promise her and explain to her, but for the moment she was preoccupied with herself, and the girl was scolded with every step she took.

For hours they sat and turned things over. What didn't come up during those evenings? Even some nostalgic tones. The son-in-law had no indulgence, not even for a single moment. He phrased his thoughts with his typical simplicity. Jews, it was no wonder people hated them. "Dealers, agents, and moneylenders don't deserve sympathy." But that didn't prevent him from joining in the conspiracy. On the contrary, among thieves he was as thievish as anyone.

At night when Bartfuss returned he could guess what had happened by the odor. If the smell of cigarettes hung in the corridor he knew that until a few hours ago his son-in-law and daughter had sat there, drunk coffee, cracked sunflower seeds. Rosa showed them what she'd bought in the dress shop, and the son-in-law spread out the stock exchange reports and pretended to understand them. Rosa admired her son-in-law, spoke about his golden hands, and she never ceased reminding them that the poor man wasn't so poor. He had a lot of money. Where was that money? That was the riddle. Even though they seldom named the riddle explicitly, its presence among them outweighed any other entity.

He had never, not even in the sweet moments of their

intimacy, revealed the secrets of his business to Rosa. Many years ago he had indeed hinted, mainly to assuage her, that they weren't poor, but he had never mentioned a sum.

"You don't trust me." She would try out her soft, feminine voice then.

"I mustn't even trust myself."

"You don't love me."

"I do love you."

That had been more than twenty years earlier. Now nothing was left of that intimacy but the cursed riddle. Since their early youth the girls had been told that their father wasn't as strange as he pretended to be: he had a treasure, and he kept it hidden. If he had given even a little of his treasure to Paula she wouldn't have to work. Yesterday, when he came home, he could tell by the thickness of the cigarette smoke that the meeting in the house had been longer than usual, they had eaten a lot of sandwiches, drunk coffee and soda, and the son-in-law had proposed a new strategy. That information, which he gathered from the remnants of the smoke, didn't make him restful.

He closed the door and slipped out of the house. The sea restored his spirit. The orangish light retreated from his field of vision. He drank his second cup of coffee in Café Rex, as usual. The café was empty.

While he was sitting and drinking he remembered Dorf. Since that bitter meeting Bartfuss hadn't seen him. "I don't owe him anything," he said to himself. But that very sentence kindled an old restlessness in him, which he hadn't felt for years. He had friends in the city, like

Dorf and like Scher, but over the years he had cut himself off from them. Scher had built a big store in the center of town, a housewares store, which he watched over diligently. Handsome Scher, daring Scher had devised marvelous plans during and after the war, but when he came to Israel he seemed to undergo some hard metamorphosis. First his looks changed, then his behavior. His face took on the preoccupied look of a man of property poring over his assets. After a while he married a hardworking woman like himself. A year later he expanded the little store, bought a building downtown. His trim physique was spoiled. He got fat and the cap he wore made him look like an old-fashioned merchant.

Scher had had good times in the forests and afterward in Italy. He had been a marvelous climber, a swimmer, and, when necessary, he could strike and slip away. In all his deeds, even the most daring ones, he showed his full self, as though he were born for acts of daring. In fact he hadn't wanted to sail to Palestine, and for a long time he put off his departure with various excuses. Finally he was drawn into immigrating.

That had been in the feverish month of July, spreading not only heat but anger. But not in Scher. The heat of Jaffa affected him with a kind of strange calm. Then no one knew the tricks that passing time would play on them. Scher lost his looks and came to resemble a shrewd merchant.

"What's the matter with you?" asked his friends, the way one talks to a sick man.

"Nothing."

"What are you thinking about?"

"I'm not thinking."

That, apparently, was the plain truth.

He had become like his forebears, cautious merchants, even assuming a kind of religiosity. At first he and Bartfuss used to see each other, remember old times, even miss them. But commiseration quickly turned to estrangement, estrangement to constraint, and constraint to repulsion. Bartfuss avoided him. Scher's big store prospered. He was elected to the neighborhood council. After a while they said he had become a party member.

Now Bartfuss had no close friends in the city.

Except for his hiding place, to which he gave a lot of thought, and except for the treasure, this alien ground would be barren. The treasure consisted of three gold bars, five thousand dollars, two necklaces, a few gold watches, a few pictures of his mother, his father's passport picture, and a small photograph, apparently from school, of his sister. These possessions were very dear to him. He devoted his most pleasant thoughts to them, as if to a beloved woman. The treasure was hidden in a narrow steel box, sealed for some reason with an ornate lock.

Several times, because of his suspicions, he had been about to remove the treasure from its hiding place. True, it made no sense to keep it in a damp cellar, open to the wind and inviting people to dig around in it. He knew that, but he still didn't take it out.

A week after he recovered from his illness they sent Paula in to talk with him. It was already very late.

"Who's there?" he asked.

"Me," said Paula, and he recognized her voice.

She was wearing a brown dress, very open at the neck.

Her hair was scattered in front of her face, and a heavy smell of perfume wafted from her.

"I wanted to talk to you," she began.

Bartfuss looked down.

"Mom suffers all the time."

"From what?" He rejected that false sympathy.

"Don't you know? Because she doesn't have enough money. She lives frugally. Bridget's grown up, and she has to be dressed." There was something too smooth in her voice. That was surely how she worked on her husband, the thought crossed Bartfuss's mind.

"I give what I can."

"Are we going to get involved in petty accounting now too?"

"What do you mean? I don't understand."

"You need rest."

"I'm healthy."

"Of course you're healthy. You look well, but don't you want to let the family in on your future plans?"

"Let the family in." That was a new expression. She had apparently learned it from her husband. The smell of ruse wafted from her. The rest didn't belong to her either. At any rate she hadn't gotten it in this house.

Not a sound came from Rosa's room. They were sitting and eavesdropping now. One could feel their tense vigilance.

"I don't understand what you're talking about."

"I mean more sharing. I'll be frank: suppose you get sick again."

He raised his eyes, fixed his gaze on hers, and said, "I don't intend to get sick." He put all his self-restraint into that sentence. "I won't get sick again. Don't worry."

His words put her off a bit, but she recovered and said, "Does sickness depend on a person's will?"

"I don't know. At any rate I don't intend to get sick."

"And what will Mom do for now?"

He knew that the phrase "for now" had only one meaning: what will she do after he dies?

He was incensed: "I'll always be here, don't worry."

Now it seemed someone was about to break in and say something. But that was a mistaken impression. They were sitting in the next room and eavesdropping. Paula made a strange feminine gesture and said, "You ought to know that Mom needs a special diet."

That was a complete lie. Rosa never complained about her health except when she needed money. She would waste the money on dresses and cosmetics. "That's the first I've heard about a diet."

"You ought to know," Paula said with a feminine drawl, "Mom is on a strict diet."

"So what does she want from me?"

"Consideration."

He knew. Consideration meant more money.

From then on they met every night, drinking coffee and eating sandwiches. The smell of omelet hung in the house until the wee hours. He knew the siege had begun, but it didn't worry him much. Their blind groping secretly pleased him.

He would spend hours at the sea. The thin sea smells thrilled his senses to the point of fainting. That was his refuge. Sometimes he would fall asleep on a bench. Not every day. Sometimes longing for his friends would beset him. One by one they had fallen away from him, but it didn't seem to be a complete falling away. When no one was near he would silently give himself over to his treasure. The thought that the treasure was lying quietly in the ground gave him pleasure like the thought of a devoted woman. For hours he would sit and daydream.

One evening on his way home he felt that something wasn't quite right with him. Once again he saw that orangish spot before his eyes, but this time it was larger, and little dark spots raced around it in circles like bugs. He went back and sat in a narrow café. A cup of tea did him a lot of good.

While he was sitting there a short, solid woman appeared at the door, dressed in a polka-dot summer dress, the kind they used to wear before the war. "It's her," he said to himself, not knowing what he was talking about. A face rose up and spread out before his eyes, but not a single name.

He sat and looked at her closely: broad, solid, her back bare and freckled from the sun, a little bowed. A full face without a trace of beauty. A few beads of perspiration here and there.

As he sat, stunned and lacking words, the name flashed through his mind like a burst of light: Theresa.

On the long trip, which had taken nearly a year, to that little camp known for its horrors, he had seen many faces, but no people. Starved, crushed into freight cars, the people had learned to ignore each other, to steal and push like beasts with the little strength remaining to them. One after another, feelings were numbed. The suffering was ugly. Except for the few visions of the end of the battle, the agonies would have been even uglier.

In one of those hidden warehouses, on the long road,

he met her. He was in his twenties, with no father or mother, already thin and longing for death. When everything was locked and dark, Theresa's face had broken through. There were many faces there, thin and tortured, but a clean light, tinged with deep blue, covered Theresa's. All that night they spoke about *The Brothers Karamazov*. In her high school, in the literature club that met in the library in the afternoon, they had discussed *The Brothers Karamazov* that year. Interest in the work was high, and they even tried to find a way of dramatizing it. Even afterward, when they had already been expelled from school, in the ghetto, they kept meeting in a cellar to read and discuss. One evening, upon returning home from the discussion group, she hadn't found her parents.

They were exhausted and beyond hunger. But Theresa remembered the book in detail, and she knew the whole opening by heart. She spoke softly, with an inner voice. For his part, he hadn't uttered a single sentence.

When day broke they didn't have a chance to say goodbye. Whips descended on them from all sides.

"Is that Theresa?" He roused himself.

"Certainly it's Theresa."

"I must get up and say something to her. Surely she'll remember."

While he was still stunned with joy, a man appeared at the door and shouted, "I don't like this place." His voice had authority, like a foreman bossing around laborers. Theresa looked at him from where she sat without answering.

"I said something," said the man, in the same voice.

"What's the matter with this place?" The proprietor mixed in, spreading out his arms as if in demonstration.

"I wasn't talking to you," said the man without taking his eyes off Theresa.

Theresa didn't budge.

Now the man walked over to the table and said, "Don't you see? Too many people. Come out to the promenade. The coffee's better, and there are cream pastries."

She sat in her place without answering.

"Okay, I'm going. You can do what you want. I won't try to change your mind." He spoke and went out. It was definitely Theresa. He had borne that night, with its long trip and human cargo, in his heart for many years. Phrases from the beginning of *The Brothers Karamazov* had secretly sung within him. Recently he had forgotten the opening, but not the tones. Sometimes those tones woke him up at night.

"You'll be sorry. I'm going," said the man, from the door.

Now her hands rested heavily on the table.

"Make me some toast and coffee," she said to the proprietor.

"What does he want out of you?" The proprietor's answer wasn't long in coming.

"Don't ask me."

"He's usually quiet," said the proprietor as he made the toast and ordered the waitress to get the coffee ready. Those little movements momentarily captivated Bartfuss's eyes. He was sunk in himself without thoughts. Now he could see only that orange spot, surprisingly changing hue.

No one else was in the café then, only shadows broke

in from the street. The fan didn't stop flapping its metal wings. She sat erect in her chair, filling it. When the toast and coffee were served she immediately put two heaping spoonfuls of sugar in the coffee and stirred it.

"Is that Theresa?" He couldn't contain himself.

Now he doubted his first impression.

"Water. Why don't you serve water?" she called without directing her glance toward the proprietor.

"Theresa," said the proprietor from his high stool, "you're clean out of patience today. Am I right?"

"I have good reason to be annoyed."

"Is it my fault?"

She didn't answer. She scraped her chair heavily as though about to draw closer to the table, which made her broad back stand out, strewn with bright-red freckles from the sun.

"He's usually quiet," the proprietor said to himself. "I'm surprised at him. Do you want more toast?"

"No." She sat in her place without saying a word. There was no softness in her silence. A kind of repugnance tightened her lips.

"Give me a wafer. I want a wafer." Her voice changed.

"Right away," said the proprietor.

He got down immediately and stood beside her the way one stands next to a mutinous creature. "Theresa," he said, "I'll willingly do whatever you want, but not when you're angry."

"He annoyed me today."

"Is that my fault? Aren't I serving you faithfully?"

"Don't talk."

"I'm a human being too. I also want a little consideration." His voice sounded false.

She dug her teeth into the wafer and chewed. Her senses became concentrated on that chewing.

A few people came in and spoke noisily. They seemed like strangers, unnerved by some misfortune.

Bartfuss rose as though to address her. He didn't do it. He turned his gaze to the door. Thick darkness blew in. He straightened himself, buttoned his shirt with a heavy, slightly artificial movement, leaned over, and said in a whisper, "Excuse me."

"I don't talk to strangers," she replied immediately.

"My name is Bartfuss. We were together in the warehouse in Dorfenziehl, don't you remember?"

"Strangers don't interest me."

"I understand. But we were together in the warehouse in Dorfenziehl. Don't you remember?"

"Strange, everyone remembers me." She extruded the words through a mouthful of food.

"But I was there. We spoke about *The Brothers Karamazov.* Believe me, I remember the conversation very well."

"This man is bothering me." She turned to the proprietor.

"Sir, please don't disturb my customers."

"But . . ." he tried to say. The words stuck in his mouth. He quickly paid without looking at her and went out.

On the way home he didn't meet anyone. His feet were light and bore him through the alleys. Here and there he took a shortcut, went around, and continued. When he opened the door he immediately knew that they had been sitting there all night, smoking, eating sandwiches, drinking coffee, and talking all the while. It was also clear that this time they had worked out a new strategy against him, in detail. Now they were all sleeping as though after a drunken revel.

Bartfuss opened the door to his room. The broad room, devoid of furniture, was strewn with nocturnal shadows, as if alarmed by his presence. Without turning on the light he took off his shoes, hung his shirt on the chair, and with careful movements folded his trousers. He immediately got under the blanket and curled up.

The thin shadows had scattered when he entered. Now they returned to the floor and immediately began to swallow up the spots of light.

7

MAY WAS BRIGHT, MILD, and pleasant for walks; momentarily Bartfuss's life dropped anchor, as it were, at that pier—not exactly a splendid pier, but one that aroused many hopes: Theresa. Now he relived that horrible journey to Dorfenziehl as he had never lived it before, in detail, with a kind of visionary devotion. Above the great, collective suffering, a point of light now shone.

Day after day he came and waited for her. The daily routine didn't diminish that feeling. From hour to hour it seemed to grow stronger within him, as though nearing a holiday. Theresa did not return. Daily he would ask the proprietor, "Have you seen Theresa?" His sole answer was, "Am I Theresa's keeper?"

He forgot about his house. He would go home, sleep, go out. The eavesdropping and looks didn't stop, but he no longer noticed them. He was bewitched by Theresa. It was a thrilling captivity, which brought his senses a new kind of arousal. Also his long walks down the beach had new meaning, vitality, a kind of preparedness.

Theresa didn't return. His anticipation became tenser. He would sit for a long time and then leave as if after a stern reprimand. Sometimes it would seem to him that it wasn't Theresa's fault. She wanted to come, but her lover wouldn't let her. The turning point in his feelings came during one of his walks, and immediately the dormant will flared up in him: to struggle.

For years he had lived in passivity and somnolence, ignoring everything. In the last year his life had been restricted to the area between his house and the café, except for the night trips to Natanya. It occurred to him that if the violent lover should come again, stand at the door, and pick on Theresa, he would rise and confront him. For a few days he toyed with that thought, and in secret he gathered strength. The matter was resolved far more simply than he had imagined.

One evening a woman walked into the café and called loudly: "Sandwich and coffee—I'm fainting." She was an ample woman and he recognized her immediately: Theresa in her earthly guise.

"Theresa," called the proprietor, "where have you been? People have been looking for you."

"Don't chatter, make me a sandwich and a cup of coffee right away." She sat at the table, her face to the street. It was clear she had arrived after a lot of running around.

Bartfuss fixed his gaze on the door, the place where a few weeks earlier the tyrannical lover had stood and voiced his threats. No one was there.

Theresa hurried the proprietor: "Where's the sandwich? Where's the coffee?"

Bartfuss sat paralyzed. Theresa's sudden reappearance,

in that very earthly figure, riveted him to his spot. He only knew one thing: he had to struggle.

Meanwhile the coffee and sandwich were served. The proprietor provoked her: "Where is he?"

"Don't ask," she said curtly.

She ate hastily. Two nylon straps stretched across her back, emphasizing its breadth.

"People have been asking for you," said the proprietor distractedly.

"Interesting," she said. "Interesting."

"I'm serious."

"Of course you're serious. Did I say anything about your seriousness?"

"You're mad at me again."

"Me?"

"I can hear it in your voice."

"I'm hungry. Once my stomach is full, you'll hear a different tune."

She ate quickly. The proprietor gave her another sandwich, and she didn't thank him. The evening light lay on the filthy floor.

For a long time Bartfuss sat and looked at her broad, spotted shoulders. Her rounded back was also concentrated on eating. In fact her haste didn't last more than a few moments. She wiped her mouth with a napkin and said, "How much do I have to pay?"

"As you wish."

"I'm asking you."

"Whatever you please. Let me be generous for once."

"And if I don't pay?"

"I won't be angry."

"I'm better off not owing anyone anything," she said, and took a bill out of her handbag.

She put the bill under her saucer and moved the cup from in front of it. "I'm going," she said without getting up.

Bartfuss gathered his courage and approached her. "Pardon me," he said.

"You're pardoned," she said without looking at him.

"We were together in Dorfenziehl, do you remember?"

"What are you talking about?"

"I'm talking about the transit camp at Dorfenziehl."

"What? You still remember all those names?"

"I remember you."

"Fine. And what do you want now?"

"Nothing."

"Then why are you talking to me?"

"I wanted to exchange some memories."

"You've come to the wrong woman. Memories don't interest me. I live in the present, the present tense."

"You've awakened a lot of good memories in me."

"Excuse me. I don't understand you. What do you want?"

"Nothing."

"Then what's the point of all this talk?"

"Don't you remember?"

"No. Certainly not."

Bartfuss walked to the cashier. He walked with an erect posture. The proprietor took his bill and gave him change. Bartfuss took the change and put it in his shirt pocket.

"What do you have for dessert?" asked Theresa.

"Pudding."

"Your pudding is never fresh."

"That's an insult," said the proprietor.

"Truth before all, isn't that what they used to say?"

"When?"

Bartfuss went out into the street. The evening light was full. He walked toward the sea. The few thoughts that had wandered through his head were now scattered. He was thirsty. Two cups of soda quenched his thirst.

He thought it would be a good idea to go to Natanya now. He stopped. The line at the bus stop was long, and the people didn't look particularly pleasant to him. He changed his mind and departed. Near the shore a few young people stood in bathing suits. One of them was doing calisthenics. The night fell, tired and mild, on the low buildings. For many hours he walked aimlessly.

When he reached home it was already very late. From inside he could hear Rosa's voice: "He's here." Immediately they all fell silent. He went into his room without exchanging a look. He quickly took off his shirt, closed the shutter tightly, and wrapped himself in his sheet.

Later he heard the son-in-law's voice: "Those traders disgust me." Bartfuss was so tired that even his son-in-law's coarse, annoying voice didn't prevent him from sinking deeply into sleep.

8

THE SUMMER WAS AT its height. The thin shadows which, only yesterday, had intertwined on the walls, also faded. Light now spread across the square, even to the gutters. Bartfuss sat in the outdoor café and the people who passed by seemed alien to him, distant, as if he had no connection whatsoever to them. For years, since Italy, they had surrounded him. Everywhere. The same vocabulary and the same gestures. Individually and collectively. If only he could not look at them. Even when he ran away to Natanya or Raanana. In the bus too, in the station, in the most distant kiosks. Everywhere the same gravelly accent, the same weary blur of people swamped by many disasters which had pressed a mask of staleness on their faces.

He had stored up a lot of disgust. But the disgust had been kneaded into a kind of thin contempt, and the contempt had astonishingly become an urge—the urge to look at them. How they eat, dress, steal a little female flesh, get tangled up. Years ago he would still have shouted, uttered all sorts of phrases that would have thundered in the air for a moment. But recently he had come to enjoy observation. For hours he would sit and rummage inside them with his eyes.

He didn't measure Rosa by these yardsticks; her, he hated. Every part of her. From year to year she changed: her face, her neck, her hands. But more than anything, the words: abundant words, or else frighteningly dry. Artificial opulence or coarse efficiency. All bound together.

Now the summer again, the lust for sleep. For entire days he would sleep, deep sleep, which would wrest him away to the green regions of his childhood. Afterward he would sit in the café for hours, drinking coffee to wake up. His awakenings would imbue his consciousness with a kind of clarity, as though his wild slumber had become transparent: he, Rosa, the children, the recurrent ugliness, debts he had not honored, words he had corrupted, all those tired people who hadn't found anything for their bodies but weariness, haste, and avarice.

"Bartfuss. It's Bartfuss. Haven't you heard about him?" These were thin whispers of abject amazement.

"What do they want from me?" He would be shaken.

"Nothing. We're proud of you." The dealers' fat faces would twitch.

"I don't want you to talk about me out loud."

"We're impressed. Aren't we allowed to be impressed?"

"Not at my expense."

They needed legends too, heroes, spendid deeds. So they could say, "There were people like that too." In fact they didn't know a thing about Bartfuss. Bartfuss scrupulously avoided talking about the dark days. Not even a hint.

Once Rosa used to nag him: "Tell me something. Just me." He didn't tell. The thought that he hadn't told her anything secretly came to please him after a while. But the dealers let their imaginations run wild, and on the strength of that they made up a mysterious Bartfuss, an immortal Bartfuss. Bartfuss was disgusted by those tales of wonder. In Italy he had beaten up any dealer who indulged in too much wonderment.

In time he stopped getting angry, making declarations. He learned to ignore both Rosa and them. True, the ignoring did him no good. He withdrew, and words he had once used withered inside him. Now he only said a word here or there, and only for practical needs.

In Italy he had sworn himself to silence. It wasn't easy to be silent at that time. The heat of the day, the drinks, gave rise, among other things, to words, confessions, arguments, and justifications. Except for the activity, the continued activity, people would have beaten each other mercilessly. But frenetic activity taught them to speak little. Now nothing was left of those dark days except twitches, remnants of nightmares, grimaces, and scraps of words. But the dealers never stopped embroidering the legend.

"Bartfuss, don't you know Bartfuss?"

"Yes, I know him. He's changed a lot. I've been watching him for years now."

Or sometimes with vacant amazement: "He's changed a lot."

He would run away from them as though from pursuers. But they caught up with him everywhere.

"There are fifty bullets in his body. How can a man live with fifty bullets in his body?"

"It's a fact. He's alive."

"Because he's immortal."

"I wouldn't go that far."

"I expect great things of him."

"What, for example?"

"I don't know."

"Stop being so annoying."

"I'm not being annoying. I'm impressed."

"So what is there to say?"

"Nothing, if possible."

There was one dealer there whose glance had the sharpness of an old hawk's. He would sit at some distance and measure Bartfuss's movements. Bartfuss knew that dealer well, but not by name. He had never uttered a word or question. His incessant stare struck Bartfuss with a kind of fear.

While the idle conversation among the merchants was withering away, the old dealer cautiously approached Bartfuss and said, "Give me a thousand pounds."

"Me?" Bartfuss was surprised.

"You."

Now he saw him from up close. His face was bony, his forehead swarthy—no different from any other dealer.

"What do you need it for?" Bartfuss restrained himself.

"Why do you ask?"

"It's proper for me to ask," said Bartfuss with a kind of chilly complacency.

"Proper, you say." The man drew closer to him.

"You're the one asking for money, right?"

"Propriety is on my side," said the man, surprisingly.

"Perhaps," Bartfuss said quietly. "But not, at least, as far as I know."

"I won't repeat my request," said the man and turned his back.

"I'll give it to you," said Bartfuss. "I'll give it to you, but first I've got to know what it's for."

"What it's for?" said the old man with a kind of bewilderment, as though asking himself.

"Why ask me for money?" Bartfuss didn't let up.

"Who should I ask?"

"There are a lot of people you can ask."

"I've known you for thirty years, since Italy, and I never allowed myself to speak to you."

"So why are you speaking to me now?"

"I won't answer that. Isn't it enough that I asked you, that I lowered myself? You need explanations?"

"That's how things are done, it seems to me."

"So you're not going to give it to me?"

"I'll give it to you gladly," said Bartfuss. And with this he began feeling in his coat pocket.

"You killed off my desire," the man said with a kind of strange bitterness. "I had momentum."

"Why didn't you talk to me before?" Bartfuss tried to appease him.

"I was hesitant, and there were good reasons for my hesitation. Now I know."

"If you'd asked me before, I wouldn't have refused."

"I hesitated. It's not easy to turn to a stranger and ask for a favor."

"You say a stranger, but we went through the war together."

"Did the war make us any better people?"

"I don't know," whispered Bartfuss.

"Don't you agree that man is an insect?"

Bartfuss lowered his head. The word stung.

"I'll give it to you gladly," Bartfuss said, and held a bundle of bills out to him.

"I'll give you a receipt."

"I trust you."

"Absolutely not. Without an IOU I won't accept it. I don't trust myself. A person has to know his limitations. I know mine. I haven't kept all my promises. I owe it to myself."

"Then what do you want?"

"To sign an IOU."

"As you wish."

"I feel hesitant."

"Don't be hesitant. You'll pay this little obligation. I'm sure. Take it."

The man chuckled, took it, and left.

Bartfuss was tired. The heat and the long conversation had weakened him. The man, as it turned out, didn't go very far. He was standing nearby. Bartfuss was afraid that now he'd come back and demand another sum from him. The sun was setting on the roofs and its full light poured onto the empty square. At the nearby kiosk, shingled with flattened cans, there was no one. The owner sat on his raised stool and looked intently at the thin birds poking around in the heaps of garbage.

Bartfuss remembered that in his long night's sleep he

had frequently used one word, repeatedly kneading it in his mouth. Now that word had disappeared from his memory. He missed it like a beloved pet.

"Coffee," he said.

The proprietor woke up from his doze and said, "I'll bring it right away."

The sea changed color, and the salt breezes made Bartfuss feel drowsy. "I'll close my eyes for a moment," he said. As he spoke the man came and stood before him.

"What is it?" he roused himself.

"I want to back out," said the man. There was the same sharpness in his eyes as before.

"Why do you want to back out?" Bartfuss found some words.

"I don't know if I can pay in time."

"Is that what worries you?"

"Yes."

"Get that worry off your chest. I won't run after you."

"I know myself very well. I don't keep my promises."

"For my part you have nothing to worry about."

"I know myself very well." The man raised his voice. "I haven't kept my promises. I'm notorious for that." Although Bartfuss understood him well, he tried to mollify him, which immediately made the man furious. Finally the man took the bills out of his pocket, placed them on the table, and said, "I won't take it. No. I've shamed myself enough."

Bartfuss tried to shout, "Leave it!" But the words were choked off in him.

The man now went toward the shore. From behind he seemed younger and almost content. A sort of blue chill passed over the surface of the sea. Now Bartfuss felt a kind of insult, mixed with old dejection. The owner of the café brought him coffee and apologized. Bartfuss, for some reason, said, "That's how it is." The owner apologized again.

A few thin shadows now fell from the café's awning and combined to form an oblong geometric shape. Bartfuss looked at the shape as if he found it quite interesting. He drank the hot coffee. The liquid didn't wake him up. An old and painful fatigue crawled along his spine.

For a long time he sat and drank with short sips. The memory of the man who had taken his money and returned it gradually lost its reality. Only the long waxy fingers, their tips eaten by nicotine, amazed him again, with the kind of amazement he felt only on the verge of sleep. Now he knew there was some minute flaw in the way he had given, and that was why it hadn't been accepted. He also remembered the man's look, the penetrating look of an old hawk. "Everything bad happens to me at the seaside." He summed up a tiresome lesson for himself. The sun got lower and lower, and its light was broken on the back of the sea. The thin dejection he had borne with him since morning congealed and became sorrow, sorrow for himself. He knew that sorrow and hated it. He immediately rose and paid and stood at the street entrance. He knew the full sun would strike him mercilessly, but he went out and continued walking, like a man who knows what debts are. The sun sank in the west, and the sea was empty. A few isolated voices, shouting, sliced through space and passed before him. While he was walking up to the pier he noticed Theresa and her solidly built lover near the railing. She was standing some distance from him. He wore a tight sport shirt. They were in the middle of an argument.

"I won't go." Her voice was clearly audible.

"What's wrong with the Budapest? It's an open, pleasant café. Everyone says so."

"I hate the people who go there."

"But you have to admit the atmosphere is European."

"What did you say?"

"I repeat, 'European.' "

"That word, if you'll excuse me, doesn't mean a thing to me."

"What would you like me to say?"

"I'm willing to go anyplace but there."

"Only with trash."

"Don't call them trash. I think they're splendid."

"I hate Jewish trash."

"I love them, and I won't exchange them for any imitation. Even the word 'Budapest' disgusts me."

"You're getting me mad."

Bartfuss stood, captivated by their conversation. He could tell their argument was a long-standing one, with no resolution. They would continue it later, in the café. There was nothing in him or in her, but nevertheless there was something touching about their quarrel. Bartfuss looked at them from a distance, impartially, as though he had finally understood some other matter: his own loneliness.

9

WHEN BARTFUSS AWOKE and rose to his feet, he felt that the loneliness that had enveloped him in his sleep still clung to him. It was five-thirty, and the blue light, clear at that hour, stood in the window. A few words, which he had apparently used in his sleep, skimmed over his tongue. Their warmth still lingered. But what had he said? He couldn't remember.

He quickly made himself a cup of coffee. The silence and his energetic preparations evoked no picture in his consciousness. Remnants of the night, which were thick at first, gradually billowed up in his brain. A thin, roomy emptiness filled him. He drank his morning coffee, and the liquid quenched his thirst. He sat at the table and tried to recall. He knew that his sleep at night had been short but stuffed full. Something of it still remained with him, faint and scattered.

In the next room Rosa and Bridget were still sleeping. The windows of the apartment were closed, and the heavy throbbing of their sleep could be felt even in the kitchen. Their forgotten existence awoke inside him for a moment and then passed away.

He plunged into the act of drinking. The coffee and the cigarette inspired him with a kind of uncomprehended hope. Something from other times. "Let's go," he ordered himself. He didn't have a great desire to go out. In fact he was still entwined in the heavy cords of sleep. But to sit there and encounter Rosa's disheveled face. Maybe Bridget would get up. That was enough to set his sleepy legs in motion. He hurried, then, to get dressed. For some reason his shoes made him feel sorry for himself. He felt that the loneliness of his sleep was about to return and flood him. "I'm going out," he said, and with a wave of his hand he drove away the turgid remnants that had wafted up in him. "Always," he couldn't stop the word. But he immediately blocked his mouth to keep from speaking too much. Inwardly he grumbled. That talking, mainly noisy, used to move him. Now he forbade it to himself.

The morning light was cold. A thin humidity spread over the road. He knew the way very well. Sometimes he managed to forget himself on it.

There was no one in the café. The owner said, "You're early."

"I'll come back later," said Bartfuss, and turned his back to him.

Near the sea he remembered that in his sleep he had held a long conversation with a tall man on the subject of ugliness. The man perfectly understood what he meant and was willing to listen. Since he was willing to listen,

Bartfuss found the right words, and he used them abundantly. But suddenly a kind of change took place in the man. His attention didn't fade, but he became impatient. He said only, "Of course." Bartfuss was sure it was an expression of agreement, but he immediately saw his error and realized it was impatience. The man had already pondered the matter years ago, and that repetition merely wearied him.

"Now we'll be quiet," Bartfuss finally said.

That seemed to please the tall man.

He kept walking. The bonds of sleep wouldn't loosen. In the crowded little cafés people had now gathered on every side. They were standing and drinking coffee. Bartfuss noted a kind of unquiet panic in their faces, which they were trying to wipe away.

Bartfuss knew every one of them, but not by name. He wanted to approach someone and talk to him. He had a lot of words left over from his sleep, warm words, ready for use, but years of silence, revulsion, and abstention had brought him close to no one. A woman was there, not young, to whose face a kind of sharp heedfulness clung. He remembered her, not her name, from Italy. Then she was still young and worked in the clinic. Once she had treated his wounded leg. He remembered: she had bound his wound energetically, but not without softness. Now a kind of thin sadness spread over her cheeks.

He walked for a long time. The massy sleep of the night before still wouldn't dissolve. In one alley he heard a woman calling out loud: "Close the shutters. The light is driving me crazy." The voice was clear and sliced through the narrow alley, but no answer came to her call.

Finally Bartfuss reached the sea. It seemed to him he had walked a long way before getting there. In fact, he had taken shortcuts. The sea stretched out, calm, without too much movement. A cool breeze blew.

The café was open, and he was glad, because now he could sit by the sea and drink a cup of coffee. In his first days he used to sit here for many hours, but later he found that the sea and the salt air made him feel dizzy. Just as he sat down a man of average height approached him and said, "I believe I know you. Help me remember." Bartfuss was surprised: "Perhaps."

"Haven't we met?" he wondered.

Bartfuss rejected the man's excessive intimacy and said, "I don't remember." But the man ignored the rejection, and in words that were full of feeling he said, "Your face is very familiar. Didn't we meet in Italy?" That direct address put Bartfuss off.

"I," said the man, "had a lot of business in Italy. Here too I have extensive business. But suddenly, I don't know how to explain it, I got disgusted with it all. To tell you the truth, I'm angry at myself."

"You mustn't be angry," said Bartfuss for some reason.

"I don't want to be angry with myself, but the disgust which attacked me during the past few months has penetrated my bones. You know what I mean, don't you?"

"I don't entirely know what you have in mind," Bartfuss said quietly.

The man lowered his head and whispered: "I invested long years of my life in business. Believe me. It wasn't easy for me. All those years after the Holocaust. Without respite. Day after day."

"And what would you like?" Bartfuss softened his words.

"To tell the truth, I don't know. Life was very good to me after the Holocaust. You could say a life of plenty. One deal led to another. What more can you ask?"

"Are you married?"

"No," said the man, and a thin blush rose on his cheeks. "But I don't lack for women."

They were silent for a moment.

"What's bothering you now?"

"Nothing in particular, to tell the truth."

"Just put that out of your mind too," said Bartfuss imprudently.

"You're right," said the man in surprise. "I didn't think of that."

"If a person has everything, what else does he need?"

"Right," said the man, and his wonder fell away, leaving indecisiveness.

Now Bartfuss was sorry for the words he'd said. In fact they weren't his own words, but evidently the ones he had used in his sleep. He said, "I take it back."

"Don't take it back," the man insisted. "You spoke the truth."

"It's easy to give other people advice."

"Absolutely not. I was hasty."

For a long time they sat without saying a word. The man's face gradually sank down to the cup of coffee. He took long, absorbent sips and placed the cup on the table. Suddenly he raised his head and said, "Let me tell you something."

"Willingly."

"Will you let me say something personal?"

"I'm listening."

"During the past year I've felt an indefinable kind of mental weakness. All these years I kept myself from talking. In Italy I was consistent and sharp. But in the past year I've been flooded by talk. Words. I don't know why. Excuse me for telling you this. I never permitted myself to tell it. For my part I don't like it when people force talk on me. I hate talk. But in the past year it's been flooding me. Does that happen to you too?"

"No."

"How do you manage?"

"I nip all talk in the bud."

"In the bud. That's marvelous."

The man put his hand over his mouth but the words welled up and burst through the dam. "I can't stand talk. Talkative people drive me crazy. But I myself, and it's my undoing, have been infected with that disease. Forgive me."

Bartfuss also felt the need to apologize and said, "I'm not content with myself either."

"How is that? After all, you imposed discipline on yourself."

"I should have been more generous. People who went through the Holocaust should be generous. Do you understand me?"

"You're right." The man grasped Bartfuss's train of thought. "I would gladly share. How do you do it?" For a moment they peered at each other.

"You look very familiar to me. May I ask your name?"

"Bartfuss," said Bartfuss.

"It's you. In Naples we used to call you Bartfuss the immortal."

"I don't like to be called that. It's false."

"No. With respect. You were spoken of with exceptional respect. They didn't shoot right at every man. They shot right at you."

"I hate that talk."

"With respect, believe me."

"I'd thank you not to say that word again."

The man lowered his head. He was still muttering, but meaningless murmurs. He withdrew like someone caught in the wrong jurisdiction.

Bartfuss was angry. Acid words were on his tongue, seeking to break out. He sat as he was, mute.

"The sea," he said. "Why did I go to the sea? Everything bad happens to me when I go to the sea."

Actually his anger was mute, late, remnants left from the previous night. He was weary and thirsty for sleep. "Let's go," he ordered himself. Without thinking about what might be awaiting him at home, he took long strides toward the hill he had just come down an hour ago.

The sun withdrew and low clouds were borne by the roofs of the houses. The approaching chill brought no fear or remorse to his consciousness. Weariness filled his limbs. The desire to curl up and shrink under a blanket overpowered all others.

10

IMMEDIATELY AFTERWARD Bartfuss thought of doing many things. The old momentum came to him surprisingly. He shook off the rages that had enervated him. Something of the smell of other, distant days came to life in him. It seemed that the brown study that had afflicted him was now dissolving. Now he would devote himself to the general welfare, he would mingle, inspire faith in people overcome by many disasters. He would no longer think of himself, his agony, but would work for the general good. He didn't know exactly what he would do, but the intention had taken root in him; the street, which only yesterday had seemed narrow and oppressive, mired in a kind of turgid staleness, now washed him like a purifying rain. No longer Rosa, Paula, and Bridget, injustice and revulsion, but a man who gets up in the morning and knows what he has to do. Wholly for the public good. For the general welfare. Now all his pleasures and pains seemed like a kind of purposeful destructiveness. Now he would belong to the public. The words imbued him with the old, thin magic of self-forgetfulness. At any rate no longer oneself, the minor sufferings that come to rest in one in the morning and don't leave until late at night. To labor. That word, too, suddenly had the odor of distilled alcohol.

Sometimes he frequented a small office known as the "H.M." or Holocaust Memorial, which had been endowed by a well-known merchant named Zunz. The money Zunz had left had long since been wasted. They no longer gave grants, there were no more congresses, but in the afternoon a few people would gather and smoke cigarettes, bring old words and concepts up from the hidden treasury. Of course there were plans too: renewed activity, an expedition to Poland, to America. Academic congresses, memorials, a new world view.

Bartfuss suddenly felt that all the men gathered there were tortured by a sharp thirst: to be immersed once again in the general good. There were a few old-time activists there, high school teachers, book-loving merchants, who alternately sounded words of hope and despair. Of course there were frequent squabbles of what is termed a personal nature.

Only upon his return home at night did he find himself involved in a difficult battle, a blunt battle, from which there was no escaping. Rosa was trying to teach Bridget how to live. But more than anything else she was instructing her to be wary of him. Not to approach him, not to ask him questions, and not to take anything from him. Bridget heeded her mother's instructions with dread and submission. The results were not long in coming. Every time he came in she would flee from him. Sometimes Bridget would ask, "What did he do?"

"You're still asking? I've explained to you already. How many times do I have to explain it to you?"

"No, I understand." She would withdraw. But Rosa wasn't content. It was important to her that her daughter understand that he was indeed her father, but that he was worse than a stepfather. Sometimes she would hush her: "Don't talk now."

Occasionally he would see her from a distance, in the street.

In the street, without her mother, she looked like an abandoned girl. He wanted to say a good word to her or give her a present, but her frightened way of standing would paralyze him completely. He would see Paula occasionally. She was cold and businesslike, and, since she'd married, very practical. Money, of course. Renewed demands and open insults.

More and more he would sit in the H.M. office. The feeling that day after day he was losing something of his being was not blunted in the office either. But it did him good to visit those men who had set aside their personal affairs and were involved in burning public issues. The thought that the day would come when he too was immersed in public affairs, without partiality, made his sadness strangely milder. Once he even heard them say, "What a good thing he's here."

One night it occurred to him that in time he might take his treasure out of the basement and bring it here and sacrifice it as an offering for the public good. Then he would stand and take a public oath that he would no longer work in his own behalf but give himself over entirely to the general welfare. Bartfuss knew that wasn't his real wish, but rather his hostility. One day he would announce to her: "Yes, there was a treasure, a good-sized treasure, but it's been given to the general good." That thought secretly pleased him the way only a stolen thought can. That hidden pleasure did not last longer than a few weeks. The arguments in the office turned to squabbles, insults. There was one thin, bitter woman there who would immobilize their squawking. She demanded absolute devotion, a change in social values, and, above all, a personal example and taking to the streets. She had been a Communist in her youth. But her bitter demands were not what made the group disintegrate. It turned out that the office had incurred heavy debts over the years: taxes, municipal rates, water and electric bills. One evening bailiffs came and seized the room, and no one opposed them. On the contrary, there was a kind of relief.

11

SEPTEMBER WAS WARM, humid, and point-less. People lay about wearily in the crowded little cafés. No activity was evi-dent. The summer, now coming to an end, poured out the doors and windows.

In one entranceway Bartfuss met Bridget. For days he hadn't seen her in the open light. She was wearing a purple dress with narrow shoulders. Her full face was struck with wonderment, like someone found in a place where she didn't belong.

"What are you doing here?" He was astonished.

"I went out."

For months he hadn't exchanged a word with her. Rosa sheltered her, mostly she sheltered her from him. Bridget's retardation was a very useful tool in her argu-ments. "Bridget needs treatment. Bridget needs to go to a private doctor. There's a new drug." Rosa developed a special vocabulary for everything connected with Bridget. Over the years he had learned to distinguish between truth and falsehood. But he still couldn't always make the distinction. Rosa would silently spin thin skeins of words in her arguments, to annoy him of course.

"What are you doing here?" he asked again.

"There's no one at home. I went out to drink some lemon soda."

It had been years since he had heard her say a whole sentence.

"And do you have money?"

"Yes," she said, and opened her right fist. A crumpled ten-pound note was lying in her hand.

"Don't you need more?"

"That's enough. I'll even get change." She pronounced the word *change* with happiness, as if the change were already in her hand.

"And what are you doing?" he asked.

She answered him with a shrug.

The light poured down from above now and covered the square. No shadows were cast. For some reason he turned his head to see whether anyone was there. There was no one, just the liquid light. Bridget, unlike her sister, had been born healthy. Even then her disability had apparently been lodged in her, but imperceptible. The girl had eaten, laughed, and cried well. Only in time, here in Israel, when she was five, had Rosa discovered the strange distortions.

First he hadn't believed Rosa. He was sure it was just an excuse for demands. Also she had sheltered the girl in a strange way. After a while the disability came to light.

"Where's Mommy?" he asked.

"She went to the clinic."

"What do you want to do?"

"Nothing."

An urge told him to stretch out his arm and touch her head. He restrained himself.

A kind of alertness was poised in her eyes.

"What do you want?" he asked.

Her alert eyes seemed to sharpen: "What?"

"I'm asking you."

"A watch," she said, and immediately covered her mouth.

"Okay," he said.

She hadn't expected an answer like that, apparently. She covered her mouth again but didn't laugh.

"Come, let's go to the jewelry store." This closeness, after many years of distance, moved him.

He walked and she stepped after him.

"What kind of watch do you want?" he said without turning his head to her.

"Gold-plated."

Now her mother's voice could be heard in hers.

There was no one in the alleys. The noon light poured straight down. Strange, for years he had passed by there without noticing the thick pomegranate bushes growing.

"Will you take good care of it?"

"I promise."

In June she had turned sixteen. Rosa had wormed a good-sized sum out of him. He wasn't sure, though, that it went to the girl. There were too many cosmetics around the house. He gave it. Rosa used far too much makeup, indecently, mainly in an attempt to deceive him.

The thought that now Bridget was with him without

Rosa inspired Bartfuss with the old joy of secret theft. But Bridget, apparently, wasn't happy. Suddenly she stopped and said: "Forget it."

"Why do you want to forget it?" He turned to look at her.

"Mommy will be mad."

"Are you afraid of her?"

"What will Mommy say?"

"Nothing. Don't mind her."

His wheedling did the trick. He walked on and she stepped after him. They walked through two alleys without exchanging a word.

"Where is it?" The words escaped her mouth.

"Not far. Right here."

While they were crossing the street she took courage, swung her body sideways into the narrow opening of an alley, and disappeared. For a moment Bartfuss was about to open his mouth and shout. The shout was blocked within him. "She's frightened," he said to himself, and something of her calfishness stuck to him.

He grasped immediately that her great awe of Rosa was stronger than the temptation he had offered. Anger floated up onto his face, and he walked on with longer steps.

He went from alley to alley aimlessly. As he walked the anger died down in him. A kind of cold calm grabbed his legs. "She's frightened." The words came back and quivered on his lips. He drank a cup of strong coffee, and the thin sensation, not a pleasant one, that always visited him after a humiliation, took hold of his head, but alongside it there was a hidden satisfaction, which he didn't understand, that he had been prevented from committing a transgression.

Years of distance and alienation had not deadened all his feelings of closeness for Bridget. Over the years he had even become reconciled to her awkward name. If he ever felt longings for part of his family, it was she, that mute and needful girl, whom they spoke of as "her," like an unavoidable encumbrance.

Rosa exploited that weakness in him and not only demanded money in Bridget's name, but rummaged around inside him, as if he were to blame for the girl's continued retardation. Bridget didn't seem to understand the tangle of ill feelings; she would repeat everything her mother taught her. That drill left its mark. She was as afraid of him as of a stranger.

His head sank down to his cup of coffee for a moment. But, irritatingly, Bridget's full, exposed face wouldn't leave his eyes, a face without a shadow of beauty. Even the quivering on her lips was like an animal's. Only now did he grasp how inarticulate he had been with her.

The noon hour passed, and he recovered and left the café. The streets were rousing from the heat, people were dashing around at the openings of the alleys, near the thin shadows. The searing pain grew ever fainter within him. Once again he was ready to march. While he was striding, he saw Schmugler, someone he hadn't seen for a year. There had been times when he felt his closeness, though that had apparently been a deceptive feeling. Short, solidly built, with a somewhat rumpled coat over his square shoulders, rather like an old-fashioned teacher or a customs official. Basically a substantial man. In Italy he had radiated firm strength. Like everyone he had been involved in trade, but his dealings had had a different kind of momentum, a substantial momentum. Even then he had had both admirers and enemies. "Schmugler," Bartfuss called out loud. "You haven't changed." Something of the old, lost liberty came back to him.

"Why change?"

"I don't know." Bartfuss was embarrassed.

"I, at any rate, haven't found any good reasons to change."

That's how Schmugler was. From his father he had inherited the demand for brief sentences.

"I wanted to see you," said Bartfuss. "So few are left, and even the few, how can I say?"

"What?" Schmugler twisted his lips.

Even in the first days after the Liberation his liking for spareness had been evident. That liking had grown into a kind of lust over the years, which had, of course, made people furious with him.

But Bartfuss was happy. Thirst for fellowship made him overstep his limits. He sat and told Schmugler everything, going into lengthy detail, but for some reason he didn't tell him much about Bridget. Bartfuss knew that intimate stories went against Schmugler's grain, but he was so avid for a kindred spirit that he couldn't restrain his tongue.

Schmugler listened without responding. The afternoon light now lay heavily on the street, without movement.

"What about you?" he asked Schmugler.

"I," he answered quietly, "have stopped talking about myself."

"I remember that you used to tell us," Bartfuss insisted for some reason.

"I don't remember."

"I remember that you used to tell us a lot about your sister, about your sister the pianist."

"I?" Schmugler's face narrowed.

Bartfuss said, "Now I find myself remembering a lot."

"Not I."

"Why not? Are you under orders?"

"There's no need for orders."

They sat behind their cups without saying a word. Bartfuss knew that Schmugler was thorough and irritable and tended to speak judgmentally, but he had apparently forgotten he was taciturn, and that every inconsequential word drove him out of his mind.

After about an hour Schmugler was ready to leave. The unexpected meeting wasn't to his taste. If something concrete had been at issue he would have spoken. Chance meetings of that sort where you sit around and reminisce, encounters of that kind, had always been hateful to Schmugler.

Bartfuss, for his part, tried very hard to tie up the old threads that had unraveled many years earlier. He was taking such pains that he wasn't cautious and used all kinds of secret words and, of course, conjured up some forbidden feelings. Schmugler sat in his chair without reacting, only occasionally mumbling his dissatisfaction. But the more he told and repeated things about Bridget, the more Schmugler's look became veiled with chill, the chill of thin glass. Bartfuss casually asked whether Schmugler had seen Dorf recently.

Schmugler apparently didn't catch the question and

made no answer. Bartfuss asked again. This time Schmugler apparently did catch the question but still didn't respond. His glassy eyes radiated a few sparks of arrogance. Bartfuss continued obstinately. Schmugler narrowed his eyes. The thin sparks of arrogance changed color and became clear contempt. Bartfuss rose to his feet, and with a gesture containing a great deal of rage, he said, "I asked you something." Schmugler apparently didn't detect the repressed rage and failed to respond.

At that moment Bartfuss was seized by force. His right hand shot out automatically and pounded Schmugler's face. Schmugler was astounded and didn't react. Bartfuss hit him again. Schmugler's heavy body fell to the bench. There was no one in the café. The owner was sitting inside, in his cubicle, reading a newspaper. The words and blows were restrained. Schmugler said nothing.

"I asked you something," Bartfuss mumbled to himself. Without looking at his victim he left.

The afternoon light was now in its full abundance. The thin shadows under the rain gutters spun lines along the houses. Bartfuss's brain was empty, as if it had been rinsed clean, but his feet were steady. The thought that in a little while his crime would be known didn't disturb him. There was no one in the street. Bartfuss walked in the middle of it, and the shadow of his body wound along with him. He was waiting for the great outcry, the piercing shout, but it was delayed.

Not until he reached the kiosk did he realize that his fists were still clenched. He drank some grapefruit juice and paid with a bill. The cold drink poured down his throat with a slight burning. Someone spoke to him and asked the time. Bartfuss answered politely. It occurred to him that he should go home and tell Bridget what he had done. Also tell her that he would be at the Rex, and that if people asked for him, they should look for him there.

The thought passed through his mind and faded out. He was thirsty and drank another glass of juice. The streets were empty. The sea glittered nearby in intense green. "The sea," he said to himself, "the sea. I'd better go to the sea." He immediately walked down a side street, and, unintentionally, he found himself once again at the corner where Bridget had run away. "Bridget. I wanted to buy her a gold watch. Who'll buy her a gold watch? Rosa certainly won't buy her a gold watch." For a moment all his senses were concentrated on that issue. He forgot Bridget's flight. Without delay he went to a jewelry store.

In the jewelry store he knew already: nothing but an Omega. The store owner also pronounced the word "Omega" with a smile on his lips. Bartfuss didn't bargain.

It occurred to him that he should get out of there. A cab passed by and he stopped it. The lights increased. In the main streets people streamed in crowds, as though after a curfew. The smell of grilled meat hung in the air. At the bus station he boarded a bus to Natanya. The bus was empty, dark, patiently waiting for passengers, immediately giving him a poorly understood feeling of relief. He made a reckoning and found that within an hour he would certainly arrive in Natanya. A woman sitting to his right in the nearby seat asked him if he was well acquainted with the streets of Natanya. Bartfuss, who was awake, alert, patiently explained how she could get to Jabotinsky Street.

More passengers slowly arrived. Bartfuss counted the

cash in his right pocket and examined the gold watch again, finding it handsome, delicate, ticking quietly. Then, not knowing what he was doing, he fell fast asleep.

The roar of the motor roused him from his doze. For a moment he wanted to stand up and get off. The bus was already on its way. He knew the road very well. But now the route seemed unfamiliar to him. He asked. The passenger next to him confirmed it: Natanya. The cool sea breeze penetrated the bus and gently caressed his neck. The bus sped lightly on its springs.

When he reached Natanya it was eight-thirty. The people hurried off the bus, and he hurried too. But he saw right away that he had no reason to hurry. He had the whole night before him.

"First let's go to the sea." He tried to make a plan. The night lights were full now. People sat and drank coffee in cafeterias. The sea breeze blew along the avenue. "There's time," he said to himself, without knowing what he was talking about. But the urge that had brought him there prodded him forward, and he didn't stop.

Thus he got to the ocean. Years ago a woman had accosted him here, and he had spent the whole night with her. Now no one was there. He took two steps back and turned his face toward the light again. "Let's go to the cafeteria first," he said in the tone of a person who has finally found his course. In the cafeteria he drank two cups of coffee. The waitress, wearing a spotted poplin dress, a buxom woman, gave him a long account of everything that had happened to her from the time she had left Russia until then. The proprietor sat in his chair and didn't disturb her. The cafeteria was empty.

The old desire to observe people, which used to soothe him, seemed to return. The woman told her story simply and monotonously. Many years of suffering had taught her how to talk about her pains.

"And you?" Her eyes touched him.

Bartfuss said that he had come there to do a little business.

The woman was silent.

That silence brought him close to his own flesh for a moment. He now clearly remembered the long bus, thirsty for distance, which had brought him here, the darkened faces sunken in their seats as if in a morbid dream. Something of that avid thirst trickled into his legs now.

The woman didn't ask.

Without any clear intention he asked, "When do you finish working here?"

"In two hours."

The indirect invitation brought a hidden smile to the woman's lips.

Now it seemed to him that he had only come here to invite that woman for a stroll at night.

No one entered the cafeteria, and the silence within its walls was full.

"I'll come back in two hours," he said, and rose to his feet.

The woman looked down in assent.

He went out. The chilly, illuminated streets gave off a nocturnal peacefulness. Bartfuss conjured up broad rooms with people sitting in armchairs listening to music. His legs dragged him along the avenue. He walked for a long time. The Admiral Café, small and decorated, was full. At one time he used to sit there for hours. The pink, modern colors hadn't pleased him, but he had liked to sit there because he had always found people arguing there, bringing up old memories, and going over things that were long past.

He approached it but immediately changed his mind. Embittered people sat around the tables. The words fluttering in the air weren't hard, just bitter. "On the contrary, what were you doing at the time?" There was no glory in that question. It had the odor of an old provocation.

Now Bartfuss was wary of getting close to people.

Traffic in the street died down. The few faces, bleary in the darkness, flew past him quickly. Old words raced about his brain, words he hadn't used in years. He was particularly irked by the word "mascara." Rosa had begun using mascara a lot after Paula's birth. That word cropped up in his brain with a truly physical power.

At a kiosk he drank two cups of juice. The liquid quenched his thirst. "Now, to the sea," he commanded himself, "now, to the sea," and he went. The sea was closer than he had imagined. The thick bushes on the shore had hidden it from sight. In the empty park the dark glory was at its fullest.

For a moment he lost his bearings. He felt light, and the longer he stood there the greater was the emptiness surrounding him. No memory distracted him. As though everything was poured into him. He felt his hands. They were icy.

"What are you doing here?" A voice spoke to him.

"Who's that?" He froze.

"Don't you recognize me? My name is Lili. Once we spent the night together."

"You're mistaken."

"I've been sitting here and waiting since nine. We made a date, right?"

When he turned his head he saw a woman sitting on the bench.

"What do you want?"

"You're still asking?"

Through the darkness he saw: she was solid, wrapped in a heavy shawl, her legs crossed in front of her.

"You're mistaken."

"I'm never mistaken," she said in a voice as clear and full as an object in the darkness.

"I'm not from here. I came from Jaffa to take care of a little business. I'm on my way back. I went out to get a breath of sea air."

"That's not true. I don't want to go into details now. But in any case you won't deny me your debt."

"What debt are you talking about?"

"Don't pretend to be innocent. You know very well."

He twisted his head as though about to turn his back to her.

"I'll make a scandal. It'll cost you a lot." She spoke softly to him.

Now he cursed his legs which had led him astray. In every dark place there were lice; here too there was no escaping them. For a moment he shook off the bonds and shouted, "I don't owe you anything."

The shout made no impression on the woman. She said

quietly, "It's going to cost you a lot." Her voice was full of assurance, which made her threat more palpable.

"This is blackmail," he said, dejected.

"Why argue?" The woman spoke to him the way one speaks to a thoughtless boy.

"Take it," he said, handing her a bill.

"You can't buy me for small change," she said in tones not lacking a sense of self-importance.

"How much are you talking about, then?"

"Five hundred."

"I will not," he declared.

"Why make trouble for yourself?" She spoke in a soft, womanly voice. "Why make a scandal? That's not a big sum. You won't miss it, but I need it. A woman like me is a natural wastrel. Believe me, I could have asked for a lot more."

"You've gone too far." He tried bargaining again.

"You're being small-minded. I'm not overdoing it, believe me."

"You won't ask for any more?"

"As I live and breathe, I shall not betray this vow."

He handed her the bills.

She took the money and folded it.

That's how the business ended. He went directly to the street. As he advanced, his senses were aroused within him. The cold faded in his legs. He no longer cursed his legs or the night. His humiliation woke him completely. He even remembered he had promised that unknown woman to come and take her out on a nighttime stroll. He had missed that date too. The lights in the windows went out one after another. Moisture blew in from the sea. For a moment he turned his head to see whether that monster was dogging his footsteps. There wasn't a sound. It occurred to him that now it would be wise to return to Jaffa. The last bus left at midnight. If he hurried he would catch it. He walked like someone who knows his way. He even took shortcuts. It turned out there was no need to hurry. The bus station was right nearby. The bus stood at the platform, ready to go. People sat inside and conversed at their ease, in homey voices. Bartfuss was glad he had thought of getting there on time. The driver got off his seat and called to the dispatcher: "I'm leaving in five minutes." That shout made no impression for some reason. The driver had only meant to hurry up a man who was standing by the wall and lavishing hugs on a woman who was not particularly young.

Only now did Bartfuss know he had been rescued. As in the old days he immediately started to plan his steps: "I'll get off at the Central Bus Station in Tel Aviv and walk to Jaffa. At this hour there aren't any buses. The streets are lit. There's nothing to fear." The relaxed atmosphere in the bus didn't fade. The people spoke peacefully, at their ease, using old words that had crossed years and continents and now took hold in the darkness. He drank in the old words thirstily, and the bus didn't linger. At twelve o'clock the driver released the brakes. The people raised their voices and kept on talking, but the speed and the sea wind soon muted them.

Bartfuss was wide awake, with transparent alertness. He had even performed a few actions. But where, he didn't remember. Since he didn't remember he said to himself: "The summer has passed and the fall has come.

I have to open the treasure and pay my debt. Loyalty has not died out. The people who were in the camps won't betray their obligations. There are sacred debts. A man is not an insect. The fear of death is no disaster. Only when one has freed himself of that fear can one go forth to freedom. For we foresaw that."

His own words and those of others teemed within him and ravaged him, and for a long time the words rolled about within his brain as if on wheels. But before the trip was over, when the racing bus slowed down and the dim lights of the big city lit the window, fatigue overwhelmed him. He curled up and the storm wafted away from his body. Tel Aviv was on the verge of sleep. Even the Central Bus Station. The buses stood in row upon row. Above the darkness rose a few scraps of murky light. He headed toward his house. Though he was walking with long strides he was unable to free himself of the bonds of sleep. He felt a kind of relief as though after prolonged pain. All along the way not a single thought disturbed him. He crossed the darkness comfortably until he reached his home. The sleeping house was startled for a moment at the opening of the door, but inside nothing moved. "What else?" he managed to mutter, and collapsed onto his bed.

12

 THE SUMMER WAS LOST as though it had never been. The siege around him got tighter. Everyone joined it. Now it seemed that even Bridget was part of the conspiracy. In fact she didn't do anything. Months at the beach had browned her face and neck. Her hair had lightened and salt water and cologne exhaled from her breasts. Rosa would sometimes prod her: "Iron, iron."

Among themselves they would concoct plans, reckon, interpret. No movement evaded their eyes. They noticed a discolored spot on his forehead. "He drinks beer." Rosa immediately found the explanation.

They didn't talk about money, but everything they said revolved around it. A kind of superstition whispered to them that the money would surely come. They had to wait patiently. And indeed, that is what they did. But sometimes their patience would give way, and they fell on his empty room as if to scour it.

Upon his return late at night he would know by the

thickness of the smoke that his matters had been discussed at length. They had sifted all the details and even poked around his room. The thin shadows on the floor could tell him that.

The sea which had been so good for him during the summer no longer excited him. Low clouds drifted over the water and agitated its blue. The wind was sharp and unpleasant. He would spend most of his time in a café or taking bus trips. Sometimes he would go far, but not yet to Natanya.

Occasionally he would see his friends, Dorf or Scher. They passed by him like puffs of wind. They also followed him. Now he noticed a kind of fear in their eyes. That feeling aroused a hidden desire to reveal himself to them, but he didn't do it: he was frightened by their estrangement.

That fall he spent long hours with Sylvia. She was a thin, brazen woman without a trace of softness. In Italy after the war she had married a quiet man with good manners, formerly a lawyer. For two years they had lived in that turmoil. Her husband even managed to start up a haberdashery, but she couldn't stand his quiet and his good manners, the way he sat at the table, smoking, resting on the sofa in the afternoon. Everyone knew he was a good man, and she herself admitted it, but his movements, his quiet, measured motions, drove her crazy.

One day when her husband returned to the shed he found a note: "I'm going. I can't stand it anymore." If her cousins had sent her an American visa she would have gone to America, but her cousins were evasive, and instead of a visa they sent her a crate of old clothes. Sylvia was boiling. She undid the bands around the crate and gave shirts and brassieres away to all comers. In Israel she had been married twice and divorced twice. She called her last two husbands rascals. She spoke of them as though they were a single person. In fact only one of them demanded that she go to work. She spoke of her first husband, though, the way one talks about an annoying brother who doesn't understand the meaning of life.

She was one of the few women who had studied at and graduated from the Hebrew high school in Zeydicz. She spoke of Jewish law as she might of a prince of ancient lands. Not to mention modern poetry. That added a kind of somber charm to all her being. She would remember an archaic expression like "the effusions of my heart," and she would laugh for quite a while, like someone who smelled some homemade prune jam. Despite the vicissitudes of her life she retained something of the arrogance of a high school graduate. Lines of poetry and mathematical formulas—all in one bundle. She had forgotten a lot, but not her sensitivity to literature, a sensitivity with the odor of watery poison. That autumn, immersed in herself and smoking incessantly, she made Bartfuss feel she had words to draw him out of the mire into which he had sunk. Her melodious speech gave him something of the fragrance of gardens, a wide world, and notions that brought to mind broad streets, parks, streetlights, and theater. She herself suffered from the heat and humidity and from the ugliness. She said it would be better for her to live in the country, among ignorant peasants, rather than here among peddlers and small-time agents. The gentiles were cruel but not ugly. More than anything else she hated the religious people, crowding around stands, and on Saturday sitting on the balconies and cracking sunflower seeds. Her great pride was that she was the only daughter of nonreligious parents.

Bartfuss would bring her chocolates and boxes of candy. The fragrance of gardens didn't always rise from her words. She had words that smelled of melancholy, pain, and anguish.

At the beginning of the war she and her parents had fled together to the forest. Those were marvelous days, days of great closeness. They ate the bread and cheese they bought from the peasants at night. That was before the ghettos, before the deportations. Great fear already stood in the air. No one knew, in fact, what havoc the days would wreak. It was short-lived joy. One night she lost her way and didn't find her parents. For a month she searched for them. The woods had taken them. Since then everything she had undergone—the flight, Italy, her marriages and divorces, Jaffa, the heat—was all a meaningless illusion.

But on tranquil nights, and there were some, she would say that in her life she had the advantage of knowing she was cursed. Most of the day she sat in her room, reading, smoking, and drinking coffee. The room was neglected and in disarray, but not without strength. A thin shadow was always present in it.

Once she had said to him, quietly but very demandingly, "I expect generosity from people like you. Simple generosity. Is that too much to ask?"

"I don't understand. Am I a tightwad?"

"Not a tightwad, but not generous."

He would bring her boxes of candy or fine coffee. Once a fancy electric kettle. She would take his offerings complacently, like something that needed no comment.

He often decided he wouldn't go to her anymore. If it were summer, he would have walked to the sea. The summer had passed as though it never were, the shore had emptied, and sea winds blew over the abandoned stalls. The people had gone and curled up at home. Coming back home at night he would find a flock of crows sitting at the table.

"He's coming," he would hear.

"Talk to him." The son-in-law would send his young wife.

"You go." The daughter would gnash her teeth.

In the end Rosa herself would appear and mutter some sentence or other, which, rather than expressing a real demand, was meant to appease the children and stop them from fighting among themselves.

The son-in-law once said: "I won't talk. I have no desire to talk with him." There was revulsion in his voice. But the riddle wouldn't cease obsessing them. Where was that big sum of money hidden? Since March not a night had passed without a meeting. They talked, dug around, forced Rosa to tell her intimate memories, but you couldn't get a thing out of Bartfuss. From day to day he grew more closed, and at night, when he showed up, wrapped in his coat, he looked like an evil porcupine.

Many ideas wandered about in his brain that autumn: to run off to Italy, or to Australia. Those ideas didn't lead to action. He withdrew further into himself, subtly, but very noticeably. Only his hearing grew sharper.

The refuge with Sylvia was no easy thing either. She would say all kinds of words to him that stung him like a bitter liquid.

"You think a lot about yourself. You think about yourself too much. Can't you forget yourself for a moment?"

"No." He tried to deny it.

"Still, admit it."

In fact he liked to observe. A kind of morbid desire for trivial details gripped him. The way people sat, bent over, kept silent, or addressed each other. These tiny sights moved the frost within him slightly. In his heart he was afraid of them and attributed it to his illness.

Once she said to him, "Why don't you think about all the things that have happened to you?"

Bartfuss woke up and said, "Me?"

"It would give you a lot of courage."

"I'm not afraid."

"I'm talking about resilience."

"I don't understand what you're talking about."

He didn't talk about his family. She didn't ask him either. It was agreed between them that family matters were fundamentally bad. People were born for solitude. Solitude was their only humanity. Family life brought you down in the end. So it was, night after night. He liked to think about the words she said to him. They seeped into him by themselves like a melody. At that time she was already very ill. Bartfuss knew she was sick, but they didn't talk about it. Sometimes she would say, "You'd better leave me alone." He would leave her and go out.

The siege at home tightened around him, but that malice didn't hurt him. The long meetings with Sylvia filled him completely.

"Resilience? What do you mean?"

"A word for yourself."

"I don't need words." Bartfuss recoiled.

"Because you're living in a daze."

Now he understood very well but still asked, as if to verify her intentions.

Sylvia explained: "Does our life have any purpose?"

"I don't know."

"At any rate I'm closer to my parents now than I ever was. My love for them is boundless."

"I too," said Bartfuss.

"And if only for the sake of that love, for its sake, which is surely a pure love. Death isn't all-powerful."

In the meanwhile Sylvia fell ill and was taken to the hospital. When Bartfuss found out he gripped his head: "Why wasn't I there?" The neighbor, an orderly woman who lived on a legacy from her late husband, told him that barely two hours ago they had come to take her away. She was conscious and didn't complain. The neighbor spoke of her as one speaks of an abandoned person who will be taken from her home in the end.

He went straight to the hospital. "I could have helped her," he said. "I had the ability to help her. Why didn't I buy her a new coffee service? She wanted one so much." But that was just a passing thought. He walked. The night lights, coming down from the windows, fell on him. His quick paces grew more and more pressed as he advanced. It seemed to him that the shopkeeper who was sitting in front of his store at that moment was asking him a question. It was merely a mistaken impression. On the way he remembered the words "if only," which Sylvia had spoken to him the day before. The sound of those words roused him from his frozen numbness.

Had she already known the day before?

Perhaps. But there had been no sign on her face.

"If I had told her that I meant to buy her a new coffee service, wouldn't that have prolonged her life?"

He was already at the hospital gate. Outside, there was no activity. The evening lights were calm here, faint and a bit oppressed.

"Who are you?" asked the clerk.

"A friend of Sylvia's."

"She was saved," he said. "Just now they informed me that her life was saved."

"That's good to hear." Bartfuss didn't find any other words.

"I," said the clerk, not without self-importance, "am pleased to make such announcements."

Now he went there every day. His days took that course. He would think about her the way one thinks about a dear friend who is moving away. In fact he knew very little about her, almost nothing. That lack of knowledge did not lessen his closeness to her.

Most of the day he would sit in the café, and at four he would rise from his seat and go to the hospital. The hours would pass before him as if borne by heavy freight cars. True, he thought a lot about Sylvia, but not all his thoughts were centered on her. Bridget, for example. Her retardation. Her face appeared to him furtively. He still didn't know whether the retardation was from birth or whether it was the poison her mother instilled in her.

Years ago, when no one was at home, he had asked her, "What would you like me to buy for you, Bridget?" She had smiled and said, "A green dress."

"I'll buy it tomorrow," he had replied.

"No." She had changed her mind, he recalled.

"So what should I buy?"

"Nothing. Nothing from you."

He knew that those weren't her words but words that her mother had planted in her, but they still annoyed him. When Rosa found out she grumbled, "He wants to buy the girl for the price of a dress."

He also thought about his friends, about Dorf and Scher and Schmugler. He still didn't know when that thick wall had grown up between them. In the meanwhile he bought a new coffee service, of the Italian kind, elegant, and which went for a high price at that time. The days passed with no changes. Everything that happened happened within him, all the whispers and scratching.

In the long waiting room he noticed a man sitting wrapped up in himself with a suitcase by his side, as though he had not come to ask about a patient but to sit. He sat for an hour, rose, and left. At first his sitting made no impression on Bartfuss, but since he came every day in the same way, Bartfuss suddenly felt a kind of affinity for him, as if he were one of his old, estranged friends.

Meanwhile Sylvia's condition apparently worsened. He didn't learn the details. They only said, "She needs a miracle." The nurse, a practical woman, spoke the word the way religious people say it. The nurse herself didn't look religious. When the man heard it had to do with Sylvia, he got up and went to the clerk's window. Bartfuss asked the man, "Are you waiting for her too?"

"Yes."

"But you don't ask about her?"

The man lowered his head and a thin blush covered his cheeks. He took a short step, then withdrew. Bartfuss didn't ask any more. That night he drank two bottles of beer and promised himself that if Sylvia only got better he'd give her a lot of money. The more he drank, the more he felt a kind of blank knot loosening in him. Late at night he went to the cashier and by mistake he paid in dollars. The waiter laughed and said, *"In vino veritas."* Bartfuss wasn't drunk, just mixed up.

The next day he went back to the hospital, and when he saw the man sitting there he asked, "Did you know Sylvia?"

The man opened his round eyes and, without turning toward Bartfuss, said, "Once, I was married to her, in Italy."

"You haven't seen her since?"

"No."

"Where did you hear?"

"By chance. I work in the accounting department of the hospital."

Sylvia's condition improved, apparently, but no one was allowed to visit her. They would meet in the hall, during visiting hours, between four and five. Now Bartfuss's day was set for that hour.

"Sylvia spoke well of you," Bartfuss told him.

The man's round face seemed to get even rounder, and he blushed all over. But immediately afterward he recovered and said, "Strange."

"What's strange?"

"Our life together wasn't a success." Hardly had he

said that sentence, when a kind of surprise descended on his face and froze it.

They got little information from within: no change, they would have to wait. After visiting hours they would sit in the nearby café and drink coffee in silence. The man seemed very decent, but mute. He would answer Bartfuss's questions with yes and no by turns, with an expressionless face. When they spoke about business his mouth opened a little. It seemed that he was freer in that space. They didn't talk about the labor camps and concentration camps, of course. Bartfuss too was silent on that matter. For hours they would sit there, sometimes until late at night. Bartfuss revealed to him that his great dream had been buried somewhere in the sands of Italy, and since then his life had been without a dream. Once the man surprised Bartfuss by asking, "How was Sylvia in recent years?" Evidently that sentence had been lying on his heart for many hours.

"As usual," Bartfuss answered.

"She had a lot of complaints about me," the man said heavily.

"You never met her again?"

"No. Sometimes I'd see her."

"She spoke well of you, only well."

"I can't change my character. I promised her to change my character, but I didn't keep my promise."

Bartfuss came to the man's assistance and said, "What could you have done?"

"I wanted to, but I didn't know how."

Since they didn't have a lot of words, they would play chess. The man was a good player.

When he came home Rosa would greet him with many

guttural sounding words. "If you had a heart you'd help your daughters. A father who doesn't support his daughters is worse than a wolf. Where's the money?"

"What money are you talking about?"

Rosa would choke with excess emotion. Sometimes Bridget would appear at the door. In her face he saw the venom her mother had instilled in her. In reality it was fear. More than anything she was afraid of him, and of the dry words he would fire at Rosa.

"This is your father, he and no other," she would say, pointing at him.

That autumn Rosa's attacks didn't make his blood boil, nor did the sinister plots they cooked up against him. He was completely engrossed in Sylvia's illness, as though wrapped in a delicate webbing.

Sometimes his feet would carry him to the sea. "I'm here and Sylvia is there." His thoughts would mumble within him the way one thinks about someone close who is pulling away. Strange, she didn't seem pretty to him even now. But he knew: the few days in her company had changed him.

While he was pondering the destiny that had bound him to Sylvia, her pedantic first husband, who came punctiliously every day to hear news, and the autumn, which cast shadows and sand on the street, and while everything seemed like a prolonged expectation to him, Sylvia departed from this world.

"Now she's better," the nurse told him, saying nothing more.

For some reason the man removed his hat, like the Christians when they hear bad news.

The two of them followed her coffin silently, and not a word was heard in the vast cemetery. It was already evening, and the pallbearers said the prayers hurriedly.

After the funeral they sat in a café. The silence they had brought from the cemetery didn't leave them. They drank coffee and smoked cigarettes. After about an hour of sitting in silence, they spoke about politics. The man said that America too would abandon us, because oil calls the shots. Bartfuss agreed with him, only adding that Jews weren't flawless merchandise either. The man disagreed and tilted his head to the side, saying: "It doesn't depend on us anymore." Bartfuss said irrelevantly, "What have we Holocaust survivors done? Has our great experience changed us at all?"

"What can you do?" The man opened his round eyes.

Bartfuss was surprised by that question and said, "I expect generosity of them."

"I don't understand you."

"I expect"—Bartfuss raised his voice—"greatness of soul from people who underwent the Holocaust."

The man lowered his head, and on his lips was a skeptical smile of hidden wisdom.

"I don't understand, 'generosity'?"

The man rose to his feet, and with an arrogant movement he turned away, as though offering his place to someone. That short movement silenced Bartfuss. "Let's go," said the man, as though giving himself an order. "Let's go," he said, and he went.

13

 AFTER SYLVIA'S DEATH no change took place in his life. He got up at the set time, drank coffee, smoked a cigarette, and sat for hours in cafés. It seemed as though his thoughts had been reduced to the most practical needs. Day and night would alternate without his noticing. Except for his dreams at night his life, inured to minor persecutions and renewed pain, would have reached the little corner from which it might simply have gone on.

For some reason he would dream about Bridget a lot, but, besides that, nothing. His daily routine, you might say, speeded up. It seemed as though Sylvia's death finally brought him to the verge of the numbness he had needed all his life.

Sometimes he would see Bridget. Her months at the beach had given her marks of maturity. Her upper limbs had grown thicker. Now she wore Rosa's dresses. They fit her. Rosa was happy. Sometimes he would see them in their warm coats, walking along the promenade, not like a mother and daughter but like two women engrossed in a conversation.

Nevertheless he felt that everything wasn't quite in order. He noticed he was coming home earlier for some reason. There was no reason. In that season the cafés were full. People sat and drank and argued. Though he himself took no part in the arguments, he liked to listen. The burning claims and counterclaims reminded him of old discussions in the youth club at home.

He would leave the café early and return home. Paula and the son-in-law seldom visited now. Rosa and Bridget would fill the rooms with their being. As he approached the door he would hear, "Get out of the way, he's coming." That sentence had been habitual with Rosa for years. Now there was a kind of urgency in her voice. When he came in, Rosa's face would be paralyzed. He would sit by the door and listen. For hours he would sit. It wasn't very useful: Rosa rarely spoke, and Bridget hardly ever uttered a sound. But nevertheless he couldn't detach himself from his place.

"Does Bridget also think about me?" Now he had no doubt about it.

Rosa apparently sensed the change. Sometimes she would curse her fate, and sometimes she would cry. But he persisted. He would come home early. Once a day he would come and stand at the corner where Bridget had fled from him. It was a rather dismal corner: an abandoned yard with a dusty fig tree, but he clung to that corner with a kind of obsession.

Sometimes he would catch himself: "What am I doing here?" Something within him drew him from place to place. Now he was a slave to his feet. Sometimes Rosa would surprise him with her old voice: "You didn't give us anything." He would give right away.

"That isn't enough."

He would add.

"And a dress for Bridget."

He would add more.

Now it was a different campaign. The regular front, which was familiar, had collapsed as though of its own doing. There was no need for demands and shouts. He would give. If asked to add, he would add. That change perplexed Rosa. What had happened to him? A kind of foolish suspicion grew up in her eyes. But not for long. She defended Bridget on every side. They went out to the grocery store together. And in the afternoon they drank hot milk. Sometimes he would hear Bridget's voice. She would ask a question and Rosa would answer her at length. He, of course, was not absent from the conversation.

The autumn had come and thin rains fell. Flocks of clouds hovered over the beach. He stood outside, next to the Rex. It was five o'clock, and he didn't know what to do.

While he was standing there a feminine shadow broke out of the alleyway. First the shadow looked like a middle-aged woman. But he saw his mistake right away. It was Bridget. The shadow approached him. He waited for it tensely. But that was a mistake too. The girl stepped aside and turned her back to him. "Bridget, wait for me!" he called to her, and without waiting he lurched forward. It was an incautious movement. The girl fled in the direction of the illuminated kiosks. "Strange," he said to himself, "she runs marvelously."

At one of the kiosks she stopped and asked the owner for protection. Bartfuss stopped, stood still, and followed her from a distance. She was panting with fear, and the kiosk owner came out to her. The girl explained to him, with gestures, that she had been innocently walking in the street when suddenly someone had leaped out of the darkness. Now he saw clearly: the girl was deaf. The kiosk owner tried to calm her down, but the girl would not be calmed. For a long time she stood at the counter, frightened.

When he got home the rooms were lit. Rosa and Bridget were sitting in the kitchen, chattering away. As the door opened they fell silent. He went into his room, took off his coat, and a feeble relief spread across his chest for a moment: this time he hadn't failed.

14

THE NEXT DAY THE light was full and chilly. Bartfuss passed from street to street wrapped in his coat. The thin, wintery shadows shimmered at his feet and reminded him of another city and another autumn. Where it was, he didn't remember. Deep sleep had wiped the illusions of the past few weeks from his heart. He only remembered the bony face of the man who had asked him for a loan. Now he was sorry about the way he had offered the loan to him. If he had offered it more generously, the other would certainly have accepted.

People passed by him, and he knew every one of them. He felt like sitting in a café, drinking coffee, and smoking a cigarette. But none of his many acquaintances seemed available. They were all streaming to the center of town now: he went into one of the small, narrow cafés he had refrained from entering for years.

He knew the woman who owned it, of course, from Italy. The war, widowhood, and bereavement had not impaired the pleasure she took in life. Even in Italy he hadn't been able to decide whether it was folly or a higher wisdom. Even then she would wear dresses with open necks. She was still young then and they called her "the innkeeper," though she didn't have an inn of her own. She sold fruit juices, and that was a new thing. In that area they had only canned goods and biscuits. Lots of stories circulated about her, not particularly modest, but nevertheless she was not held in contempt.

No one was there, and the woman, sitting at the counter at that moment, called out loudly, "A good cup of coffee, that's what you need, right?"

"How did you know?" Bartfuss was amazed.

"What do you mean? It's written all over your face."

"What's written on my face?" He was drawn on by his tongue.

"Your face tells me that you have an urgent need for a good cup of coffee and a good cigarette. And I can provide you with all that. I'm glad I can offer it to you."

"Do you remember me?" Bartfuss whispered.

"Of course I remember you. I remember you from the transit camps, and afterward you were in Italy, first in the north and then in Naples. Am I mistaken? Correct me if I'm mistaken."

"No, you're not mistaken."

"You even drank juice at my place."

"Excuse me for not coming until now," Bartfuss apologized.

"Why apologize?" she said. "There are good reasons to come to Clara and also good reasons not to come. I don't blame anyone. I learned not to blame anyone."

Now she spoke about herself, in the third person. From what she said you could see there really were two Claras, a selfish Clara who wasted most of her money on cosmetics and fashionable dresses; and, alongside her, another Clara, a hidden one, whose heart went out to anyone who came near.

Bartfuss imagined that in her voice he heard the old softness he used to hear in peasant houses. She told him how she had managed to overcome fear.

"You no longer fear?" Bartfuss asked in surprise.

"No. Not in the least."

"How did you manage?"

"I'll confess," she said. "Cognac helped a lot."

"Did you also try other drinks?"

"Of course. Only cognac was really good for me. Two glasses in the afternoon."

"And you keep it up?"

"Of course, depending on the season of the year."

Bartfuss held her and kissed her.

There was no one in the café. The wintery shadows sneaked in from the rear entrance and reminded him of a house with a wood-burning stove.

"Thank you."

"Think nothing of it. If you overcome fear, everything seems different. Completely different. Fear is the great enemy of mankind. If we overcome fear, we overcome our bestiality. But you don't drink?"

"I drink straight vodka."

"There's no comparison. Cognac has a different effect. It works directly on fear. Your head stays clear."

"Weird things have happened to me this year," said Bartfuss for some reason.

"And you know how to ignore them?" She grabbed the sentence out of his mouth.

"No, to my regret."

"Cognac teaches you how to ignore things. We need the power to ignore. Cognac gives you that power. I learned that on my own flesh, I might say. I only have ties to my father and mother. I am even capable of praying to them."

"What?" He was stunned.

"They've become so close to me, so understandable, and that's the only thing that gives me the strength to live. Knowing that someone in the Upper World loves you."

"I understand." Bartfuss lowered his head.

"I speak to them very freely, as if they were here, as if they were drinking coffee."

She wanted to add something, but people came into the café and filled it. Bartfuss felt that those familiar and practical people were liable to spoil the ray of light that Clara had shone upon him. Now he was afraid of losing that feeling. Without saying, "I'm going," he got up and went.

The narrow, empty streets now flowed near the shore without any color. The early winter cast traces of its darkness on everything. The shore had emptied, and a cold wind wandered among the vacant stands.

Bartfuss didn't notice all that. He was alone with himself, swept along in a kind of great surge. As if he had cast off the anchor which had bound him to the murky seabed all these years. As in the past, he suddenly knew what he had to do, to be generous and not stingy. As he went on, that surging movement bewitched him. It seemed to him that he possessed a good slogan which he had to proclaim.

The wind blowing from the sea made his senses teem. He wanted to be close to the people from whom he had distanced himself. He went by low houses that he hadn't passed in daylight for years. Sometimes at night he used to drag a woman there. The narrow streets were empty, and the people who happened along his way were strangers. "I'll have a glass of cognac," he said as though drawn by a spell. He drank at a kiosk. The two glasses did their work quickly. His legs felt light. True, even now some scattered patches of ugliness and unpleasant-looking grimaces failed to evade his eyes—but they were powerless to cloud his spirit. He went from street to street, from one cold pocket to another, without deviating.

As he walked on, his thoughts grew fewer, blurry, and evaporated within him. The old, hidden desire which had tortured him in secret for years returned and overcame him. If a woman had come his way he would have dragged her into one of the entrances. There were no women in the street. It occurred to him that if he went on he'd certainly meet a woman, and maybe at the end, near the dock, there was one waiting for him, broad and comfortable.

While he was wandering about, Bridget appeared. She was wearing a red winter coat that Rosa had bought for her two years earlier. Excessively red, the coat made her look clumsy. Since he'd seen her last her shoulders had gotten broader. For a moment she recoiled, but she recovered and said, "I went out to see the rain."

"Aren't you cold?"

"No," she said. Stupidity and wonderment filled her face.

"It's cold today," he said, and felt muteness cutting his lips.

"I'm not cold," she said.

Bartfuss buttoned his coat and turned his head to the right. When he saw there was no one, he lowered his eyes and said, "Let's get away from here." A smile broke from her full face.

"What would you like to drink?" he asked, the way he used to when she was still a little girl.

"Coffee," she said.

"You drink coffee?" He was surprised.

"I've been drinking coffee for years." Her face expressed tranquility.

He immediately thought of taking her to the Rex. But he rejected that idea. A lot of people knew him in the Rex.

"Why did you run away from me?" He surprised her.

"I was afraid."

"Who were you afraid of?"

"Of you." Her visible dumbness astonished him. He chuckled.

"And you're not afraid now?" She opened her mouth wide. A different kind of stupidity, which he hadn't yet assayed, broke out on her face. But she said, "Now I'm not afraid of you."

A few weak lights broke through the clouds and lit the empty square. He felt a kind of embarrassment next to his overgrown daughter, an awkwardness not devoid of strange pleasantness.

For a moment he thought of getting rid of her.

She followed him the way a woman follows a man who

has motioned to her to come with him. She was tall next to him and took tight little steps.

Now he was afraid of himself, of his silence. He turned to her and said, "Why did you go out?" He spoke as though to an irresponsible creature.

"I was bored."

"What did you expect to find in the street?"

"People."

Now he knew that he couldn't get rid of her without a drink. There were many cafés in town, and in every café there was a quiet hour, but he couldn't think of a café where he could sit with Bridget. Seeing no other alternative he entered the Mandarin. He knew he should talk, but words had gone dumb within him. Bridget sat straight up in front of him. Her face was young, but her eyes were dull, her breasts were full, and her mouth open. In Italy he found ones like that by chance, near the beaches. Girls who had no will of their own, only a kind of bewilderment. He would drag them onto the sand or into an abandoned house.

Bridget asked, "What have you been doing?"

"Why do you ask?" He was surprised.

"I don't know." She withdrew. There was feminine curiosity in the sound of her voice, probing and stealthy joy. He sat and drank, trying all the time to drive out the feeling of closeness he felt for her. It was a kind of blind and sturdy feeling that he mainly felt with women of that mute sort.

"Let's go," he said, and stood up.

"Where?"

"Let's go," he repeated.

He pondered and found that the beach near the Mandarin was dark and furrowed with trenches, and it would be better to go out the back door, which was lit. The darkness of the sea was always baneful to him.

She put on her coat and followed him. Now it was clear she would go anywhere he led her.

As soon as they got out he lowered his eyes and said, "Go home," the way he had done to a woman once.

Bridget wasn't alarmed: "Why are you sending me away?"

"It's night, late already, you shouldn't wander around at night."

She didn't plead, as though she knew her strength at that hour.

"Go home." Again he drove her away from him.

Since she didn't react, only stood there, he took her arm and, with a very forceful shove, he pushed her into the darkness. The darkness was thick, and they cut through it in silence. For a long time they walked, clinging to each other. An old curse that he hadn't used for years burst from his lips. "What do you want from me?" he pestered her.

"Nothing at all." She apparently felt secure at his side. Her heavy limbs throbbed softly.

They cut through in the direction of the shore. The dark, abandoned houses passed by one after the other. Through their entrances you could hear the din of the sea. Now it seemed he was about to push her in, the way he was used to, but he, for some reason, made a broad motion as though offering that dark landscape for her contemplation. She bent over like an animal sensing a lower, narrow opening.

"Don't go in," he said.

Her back responded immediately and straightened. He used to bring the heavy, mute women here. They would walk quietly with him, saying nothing, as though they knew what was demanded of them. He had never seen these paths in daylight. But at night he stepped with assurance, almost gliding. This time, apparently, he hadn't estimated the distance right, or had gone astray, and the place seemed narrow. "Where does this go?" he asked, and again he started cursing, emitting all sorts of mixed-up curses, little more than a confused eruption of words. She clung to him with her whole body.

Near the sea she tripped. He suspected she had tripped purposely, but he saw his error immediately. Her face, lit by the sea, expressed dread.

"What happened?" he shouted.

"My leg."

Her feet were wet from the sand. He quickly took off her shoes. The smell of sweat and perfume wafted up from her lower body. She spread her legs and leaned on her hands. She had twisted her left ankle. The pain was sharp, but she didn't cry out.

He fell to his knees and began massaging the length of her leg. She didn't resist. Her face narrowed. Her pain hadn't abated, but he was no longer confused. He wanted to lift her in his arms against the facade of the kiosk. But she was ponderous and awkward and sank down like a heavy sack. For a long time he stayed on his knees. It occurred to him that she wasn't all that stupid, and maybe she was testing him. She was lying on her back now with her eyes closed. He got to his feet and shouted, "What do you want?" Hearing his voice she raised herself on her two hands and a muffled bray came out of her mouth.

The sprain wasn't that severe, and she stood up. He helped her. For a long time he dragged her along the slope toward the illuminated kiosk. There was no one near the kiosk, and the voices coming from a distance sounded like whispers. He tried to console her, but he didn't know how. At the kiosk he bought two chocolate bars and a bottle of cola. She sat on the stone wall and gobbled them down without saying a word. The pain left her face.

"Who's she?" asked the kiosk owner.

"My daughter."

"What happened to her?" He showed a shallow interest.

"She twisted her ankle."

A thin rain fell and its drops pinged on the tin roof.

The kiosk owner asked, "What's her name?"

"Bridget."

"What kind of name is that?"

The kiosk owner's questions and the noncommittal answers that slipped out of his mouth suddenly made Bartfuss gloomy.

"Let's go," he said.

To his surprise she stood up.

He brought her to the door of the house and said, "Go inside." He didn't want to stand face to face with Rosa now. A kind of sharp thirst passed though his mouth and settled in his chest. He thought that if he could get rid of Bridget he'd board a bus and in one breath he'd make it to the city center and have a drink there. She stood by the entrance but didn't go in.

"Why don't you go in?" he whispered.

"I'm afraid."

"Who are you afraid of?"

"I'm afraid of Mommy."

"There's nothing to be afraid of."

"When I come home late, she yells at me."

"I'll come in," he said, and burst inside.

Rosa was silent, not uttering a sound. Bridget took off her coat and said, "It's raining out." Bartfuss opened his room. Through the door he heard Rosa's questions. Rosa asked, "Where were you?"

"I took a walk."

"And why were you late?"

"I don't know."

"What did you see?"

"Nothing."

"Where did you meet him?"

"Outside."

"Why do you talk to him?"

"I didn't talk."

"You're lying."

Later, when no more sounds were to be heard outside, and the heavy door separating them was also closed, Rosa roused herself from her silence and said, "Why don't you tell me the truth?"

Bridget didn't answer.

"Don't I deserve it?"

"What?"

"To be told the truth. Who raised you? Who educated you? Now you won't tell the truth to your mother?"

"I told." Bridget's voice trembled.

"You told me, but not the truth. You can lie to everyone, but not to Mommy. You were a very sick girl, all those years you were sick, and I gave you my whole life. I had nothing in my life. He pays no attention to me. All those years I had to beg from him for you. I don't ask for gratitude, I just ask one thing—that you tell me the truth."

She spoke and burst into tears. First it seemed to Bartfuss that Bridget was crying, but he realized his error right away. It was a bitter, torn weeping, containing sadness and shame.

"Nothing, believe me," Bridget repeated that sentence monotonously.

Rosa didn't stop weeping: "Everything falls on me. Everyone falls on me. As if I were a barrel."

Bartfuss heard the word "barrel" clearly, and it made an impression on him. He moved to the side.

"I'm going away," Rosa said in a kind of stupid tone.

"Don't go," said Bridget. "I'll never leave here, ever. I promise."

"But why did you go tonight?"

"I don't know. But from now on I won't go."

Once again he couldn't tell Bridget's voice from Rosa's, as though the two voices had mingled with each other.

15

ON OCTOBER 4, IN THE late afternoon, on the sidewalk in front of Café Rex, Bartfuss met Schmugler. First he tried to walk around him and step aside. It was too late. They stood face to face. Schmugler had gotten thin. His narrow, long face seemed even more stretched. He held a briefcase which appeared to be full of documents.

"Will you forgive me?" Bartfuss asked breathlessly.

"I? For what?" Schmugler stepped back a little.

"For hitting you."

"What do you need my forgiveness for?" Schmugler recovered himself.

"I regret it."

"I hope not for religious reasons."

"Religion has nothing to do with it. You know I'm not a religious man. In my youth I *was* religious, but years have passed since then." Bartfuss hurriedly laid out the facts for him.

"It's easy for me."

"So you do forgive me?"

"I said so."

"Why are you hesitant about saying it right out? Is it hard for you to say, 'I forgive you'?"

"If you find it necessary, I can do it easily. Though I don't like declarations. Declarations and orders derive from religion."

"In your heart do you forgive me?"

"I see you need it. Take my forgiveness, then."

Bartfuss knew Schmugler wasn't doing it maliciously. That was his way—morbid precision, excess awareness, complicated pain. In Italy he had already been hated. But in recent years that complex had taken over absolutely. His friends had withdrawn from him. Except for his younger brother, who had gone to America after the war and who sent him a monthly remittance, he would have gone hungry. In the past year he had also quarreled with his brother, once again over a single word which Schmugler had insisted on.

Though the brother hadn't stopped sending the remittance, he had reduced it significantly. Since then Schmugler had lived penuriously, ostracized—and even people who once liked him had become distant. But he persisted, especially in matters regarding words. In Italy he had refused to accept dollars from the Joint because the director of the Joint was a religious man and had given out prayerbooks with the money. Schmugler regarded that as a subterfuge and refused to take it. Ultimately he never got a cent.

"You're making people angry at you. What do you care? It's only a word. No one means it seriously." His friends and relatives wheedled him. But it was no use. The spirit that possessed him wouldn't loosen its grip, even when he needed the money the way one needs air to breathe.

Bartfuss was ill at ease. Since he had hit Schmugler in the face he had been looking for a way to get to him. It wasn't a systematic search. There had been days when he hadn't thought about him, but sometimes on the shore he imagined he saw him, though he knew that Schmugler wasn't in the habit of strolling about. Now that Bartfuss had been forgiven, he no longer knew what to say, so he said, "Thanks."

"Why thank me?"

"To express my feeling. Did I hurt you again?"

"You know I don't like polite gestures. Excuse me for using the word 'I' so emphatically."

"Will you permit me to invite you to join me for a cup of coffee?"

"For a short time, gladly."

Now he sensed the idiocy of his words. Oddly, Schmugler didn't act harshly toward him. He put the briefcase under his arm, a movement that gave him the air of a clerk returning to the office after lunch. Bartfuss was about to tell him about his most recent shame, but he immediately recalled that what had happened between them had happened after a similar confession. Schmugler hated confessions.

In Italy they used to talk. Then, in the great confusion, Schmugler had quietly worked on himself. While everyone else, big and small, was flooded with life, he would sharpen his words with cruel strictness. Even then he had aroused everyone's hatred. In recent years the hatred had faded, but not the repugnance. Schmugler suffered in silence, with a kind of hidden arrogance.

They sat and drank silently.

To Bartfuss's astonishment, Schmugler opened his mouth and began talking. He told about the younger brother who had emigrated to America, and about the quarrel between them. Everything, of course, because of a single word. The younger brother had quickly adapted to American ways, even joined some Orthodox community, and gradually his letters had begun to sound self-righteous. At first Schmugler had tried to ignore them, but in time he couldn't and wrote back. The brother was insulted and reduced his support, though he kept sending letters. In time his self-righteous remarks became arguments, even demands. In one of his letters he remarked that it was only proper to add the phrase "God willing" to every expression of a wish. Schmugler sent back the remittance, and since then their relations had been broken off. Now he was working as a watchman in a lumberyard. He had enough to live on and was even saving to send back what he had received from his brother, a thousand dollars.

Schmugler spoke in a monotone now, like someone recounting a long, embarrassing story. Some of the tension left his face, and for a moment it seemed as though he were once more sunk in the search for words, this time for a suitable description. He did describe the large lumberyard at length, where he stood on watch during the long nights, the beams which arrived from afar, the porters and agents, and about the man who owned the lumberyard. Now one could hear his surprising faculty for precise observation. He often used the word "beams," so that Bartfuss too felt the marrow of that word. Suddenly, out of context, he said: "Enough talk."

"Where are you going?"

"To the lumberyard. A man must return to his lair at night."

"Won't we see each other again?"

"Of course we'll see each other," said Schmugler with a broad gesture.

Bartfuss stayed where he was. A kind of distant dread fell upon him, like the days in the forest. Then too they had asked, "Won't we see each other again?" Now Bartfuss felt a kind of thin but very firm closeness to that tortured man. As though a task beyond his strength had been imposed upon him, and he had been steadfast. Now he was on his way to the lumberyard, to pay his debt to his younger brother.

"I wanted to say something to you." Bartfuss tried to detain him.

"Can't we put it off until another time?"

"I wanted to say something to you."

"You're putting me in a difficult position," said Schmugler. "I have to get to the lumberyard. At four-thirty I have to be there. I have just five minutes. We'll surely see each other. We must see each other." Those words had a placating sound, and for some reason they soothed Bartfuss's feeling of shame, and for many hours afterward he strode through the empty expanses without exchanging a word with anyone.

16

THE NEXT DAY HE slept until late in the afternoon. Outside it was bright and cold, and no memory throbbed in his brain. He crossed the slope and stood by the shore. The barren shore, greenish at the ends, moved him. He wanted to stand there looking, but the wind slapped his face, and he moved on.

For a long time he walked along the coast without turning right or left. Pink lights shone on the sea, giving the water a chilling air. Years ago he had met Schmugler not far from there and they had held a difficult but instructive conversation, which was like the making of a kind of contract. Schmugler, as was his wont, insisted on every word. Though they hadn't parted angrily then, Bartfuss had been apprehensive about meeting him again until the day when he had met him and hit him. The argument had turned on two words, *mercy* and *generosity*. Schmugler had been very scornful of the word *mercy* at that time. He even demanded the prohibition of its use.

As for *generosity,* he had more than a few reservations. Bartfuss recalled that someone had told him, in another context, that the words that had served us before were now prohibited, like a forbidden indulgence.

When he entered the café he knew that a few days earlier a strange closeness had existed between him and Bridget. That knowledge frightened him for a moment, and he sat down hurriedly. He ordered coffee and lit a cigarette. For a long time he sat there, drinking two cups of coffee and watching the thin lights penetrate through the window and scratch thick lines on the floor. There were few people in the café at that time. They seemed sunk in themselves, and their opaque faces expressed a kind of annoyance. Bartfuss tried to remember, but no memory occurred.

Later an argument flared up, not really an argument, just exchanges of words which smashed in space and sounded mainly like rhetorical questions. They had no focus, and nobody looked for one either. The new waitress, who was a bit thick, tried to make an impression on the people sitting there, saying things in a German accent. She didn't manage to catch anyone's eye. They needed hot coffee more than anything else then. Nevertheless, before he stood up to pay, Bartfuss managed to catch the following short sentence: "Everything in its own time, friend." He had thought to turn to the right. The cold evening lights turned blue and the winds whistled. He buttoned his coat.

As he walked along he saw Marian. He hadn't seen her for ages. Now she appeared, short and wide, next to the solid wall. Her shadow was longer than her body. He approached her. Her face pulled into the collar of her coat, and she stepped back.

"Don't you remember me?" He spoke to her.

"No," she said, and a smile ignorant of all emotion spread on her face.

Bartfuss remembered that smile: innocence and stupidity packed together.

"My name is Bartfuss, do you remember me?"

"No," she said, and she turned aside toward the wall.

At one time they had spoken together a lot. She had been thin and pretty. The many years of war hadn't impaired her stupidity in the slightest. A man could say to her, "Come, I'll give you a box of candy," and she would go with him. Even adolescents could seduce her with inconsequential things. Among others she was accosted by idiots, old men, melancholics, and plain idlers.

The Joint doctor knew her well and scolded her every time she showed up at the clinic. They put her in detention several times, and once they even sent her to a remote Italian village. She would come back, and everything would start again.

The doctor: "They seduced you again?"

Marian: "They promised me a box of candy."

The doctor: "And you believed him?"

Marian: "Yes, I believed him."

The doctor: "How many times do I have to explain it to you?"

Marian: "I refused."

The doctor: "Get out of here. I don't want to see you."

Marian: "Why are you kicking me out? I'm not to blame."

That's how it would be, at least once a week.

Lots of stories circulated about her. They said she had a duffel bag full of candy boxes, others said she also collected toys.

She came to Israel with everyone else. In Israel her way of life hadn't been changed at all. At first she had again been surrounded by boys, old men, and idiots. After a while they had stopped using her, and she found refuge in an old Arab house, on the ground floor. Her face lost its soft smile, and some lines of bitterness were engraved on her lips. Bartfuss would give her a little money or a box of candy. She wasn't used to free gifts and would run away from him. In Israel too he had liked to observe her. She would walk barefoot on the seashore or sit with her legs crossed. People stopped bothering her; she became a shadow among the other shadows of the place. After a while she got fat, her face swelled up, and only a few thin scraps were left of her youthful beauty.

"Don't you remember me?" he said. Apparently it was important that she remember him at that moment. Marian tightened her lips. She was moved to be unexpectedly addressed, but her memory betrayed her.

"In Italy." Bartfuss tried to offer her a hint.

"I was in Italy too." She grabbed at that word.

"And you don't remember me?"

Something of her former beauty seemed to return to her face, but she couldn't make herself remember. Bartfuss knew that his question was fruitless and evil, but still he stood, awaiting a reply.

When none came, he asked again, "What are you doing?"

The question brought a blush to her face. She pulled her coat tight and said, "Nothing, nothing."

"You aren't sad?"

On hearing that question her face broadened, and a smile broke out on her mouth.

"It's winter, aren't you sad?" he pestered her.

"I have a warm coat," she said, and touched her coat.

Bartfuss didn't remove his gaze from her: "What are you thinking about?"

"Me?"

"Yes, you."

"I don't know."

Now suspicion rose to her face. She surveyed the street, the houses around her. There was no one.

"Where are you going?"

"I went out."

"Where do you mean to go?"

"I don't mean to."

Her direct answers riveted him for a moment. He wanted to detain her and ask her more and more, as if to see through some matter that he himself couldn't quite grasp.

"And you remember Italy?" He pushed the wheel back.

That question confused her. She crossed her hands in the sleeves of her coat, hunched her shoulders, and with a movement betraying loss of mind, she said, "I remember."

"So why don't you remember me? I used to give you lots of candy."

"You?"

"Me."

"There were a lot of people in Italy. I don't remember all of them."

"Not everybody gave things to you. I gave things to you." His voice carried a threat, and she was frightened.

"What can I do? I forgot."

But it was very important to Bartfuss that this miserable, stupid woman remember him and thank him for what she had received from his hands, for nothing in return, the candy. If she had admitted that he had given her boxes of candy, he would probably have left her and gone on his way. But she didn't remember, and, on that murky evening, it mattered to him that this woman should thank him. She didn't understand what he wanted and stood near him, frightened and confused.

"At least say 'thank you,' " he said.

"I'll say it, I'll say it," she said, as her face became more and more wrapped up in fear.

In the past, when boys would fall on her, she would run for her life, to the sheds, and there she would ask protection of the refugees. But now she was fat, her body was awkward, and in her winter coat her legs looked as though they had been cut off.

"Strange," Bartfuss said to himself, perhaps grasping the stupidity of his action; but another power, an inner one, drove him on relentlessly.

For a moment she was about to beg for her life. She opened her coat and showed him her left leg. It was swollen, blue, and bandaged up to the knee.

"What are you showing me?"

"I didn't want to show it to you."

"If you don't want to show it to me, why are you showing it?"

"I was at the doctor's this morning. The doctor told me I should be careful and not get my foot wet. He himself bandaged the wound on my knee. He also gave me some salve."

"Are you doing what the doctor ordered?"

"I'll do it before I go to sleep."

"What do you eat at night?" he asked, irrelevantly.

"I mash up an apple." Her frightened mouth opened in a narrow smile. "I get apples free from the grocery store."

"For free, you said?"

"I swear, for free."

"From now on don't accept things for free from him. He's a bastard, you hear me?"

"He gives them to me."

"Don't take things for free anymore," Bartfuss said, and pulled out a roll of bills. "Use this money to buy things from him, only with these bills."

"It's too much," she said, grasping her head with both hands in alarm.

"It's not too much. It's just what you need."

"They'll steal my money. I don't know how to keep money. I never had so much money."

"Take it," he ordered her.

"I'm afraid."

"I tell you, take it, and don't be afraid. You mustn't be afraid."

He could tell she was trying to put out her hand to take it, but her hand froze. She stood where she was without moving.

"Take it." Bartfuss raised his voice at her. "From now on you won't take apples from the grocery store for free.

Don't take anything for free. If you understand what I'm telling you. Now, put out your hand."

The hand stuck to her side.

"Put out your hand," he ordered.

"I can't," she said with a voice close to tears.

"Don't be afraid anymore," he said. He pulled her hand toward him and stuffed the bills into it.

The paralyzed hand apparently intended to grasp the bills, but the bills didn't stay in the hand. They fell out and flew away. Bartfuss, panicked, hurried and gathered them up. While he was hastily picking them up Marian recovered her frozen senses and started running away. Her short legs didn't take her far. She ran like someone with bound legs, and she tripped. Bartfuss easily caught up with her. He thought of stuffing the bills in her pocket, but she, for some reason, blocked her pockets with her hands. For a moment he looked at that miserable woman, then he slapped her in the face and shouted, "Stupid."

She didn't react. Since she didn't react, he slapped her again. Marian fell down, and he shouted, "You won't take things for free from the grocery store anymore. In the grocery store you have to pay. Never take things for free." She lay on the ground, her legs quivering, and she said nothing. He crumpled the messy bundle of bills and stuffed them in her pocket. As soon as he moved away she began to scream.

Bartfuss crossed the open area quickly and headed toward the sea. A few thick spots of darkness lay on the water. It was quiet as if before a rainstorm. "You don't take things for free in the grocery store," he muttered. For a long time he could hear her shouts, but as he got farther away, they grew weaker.

As in the past, in the great days of Italy, when everything was wide open and people dealt powerfully with each other, he crossed the road. As though he had loot in his hand. He felt no weakness or remorse.

Now the evening spread out before the houses. The air was very humid. Except for the cold, which was soaking into his legs, he would have kept on, but the cold forced him to go back to the buildings and from there to the Rex. In the Rex, people were sitting and drinking coffee. He took off his coat and sat in a corner. The waitress brought him a sandwich and a cup of coffee. He had no will other than his desire to drink and eat. The few lights, scattered over the tables, distracted him. The hand which had slapped Marian in the face a short time ago was warm now and enjoyed contact with the sandwich. He sat and fixed his gaze on the new waitress. She was a short, nondescript woman, and her Hungarian-German accent added nothing to her charm. As on the previous occasions, she tried to be pleasant to the guests.

Afterward too, on his way to the apartment, he felt no revulsion or pain. His limbs were warmed up properly. When he entered the house Rosa and Bridget were already sunk in sleep. In his room there was no sign of a strange hand. Only when he drew near the bed did he feel that that mighty sleep, that full sleep, which he had been struggling against for years, had gathered strength, and now it was about to spread its iron web over him. He managed to take off his shoes and socks, to put his shirt on the chair, to look about the naked room, and to say a sentence to himself that he had heard by chance: "From now on I shall remove all worry from my heart and sleep."